RUMORS

RUMORS

Stephanie Abrams

To order additional copies of this book, contact:
Xlibris Corporation
1-888-795-4274
www.Xlibris.com
Orders@Xlibris.com
127154

Dedicated to

those people who have learned not to wag their tongues

and their dogs who would never carry a tale.

CHAPTER ONE

HERBERT HOLMES HAD had enough. He had made a fortune as the sole proprietor of his company, Mr. Bodyparts. He fell into business as an orderly at the hospital morgue. Homeless people who died in the hospital usually had no identification, no one who cared, no one to claim them. Herb used his street smarts and made some connections with local university medical schools that needed cadavers and body parts for training medical personnel. A business was born.

Herb's street smarts lead him to opportunities. Through his street friends, Herb was connected with a number of organizations that, on a fairly frequent basis, could provide him with a body as a result of their own "business endeavors." In cases like this, Herb got paid on both ends: once to accept the body from the donating organization, and again by the medical institution making the purchase. The payment from the first group was infinitely greater than the payment from the second, which was always in cash, often paid in a brown paper sack in a dark alley or railway station. And only the payments from the medical schools were reported as income.

Herb's business provided him, and whoever was his current companion, with a very comfortable life. But even Herb had to admit that his product was a bit depressing, and he had had enough. He had plenty of money tucked away in all the right places and the time had come for him to live a clean life.

Herb's plan was to run a sale, clear out his inventory, and move on to where the air is clean and life is good. To that end, Herb let the medical institutions know that he was having a clearance sale and going out of business offering them some serious discounts for orders placed for delivery at once. He found an incredible house in Aspen selling for seven figures and paid $350,000 in cash and the rest under the table to the owner. He put his home in Short Hills, New Jersey, up for sale. He was ready to move on.

The only problem Herb had was he had a little bill collection to take care of before he shut down his operation. One of the accounts receivable items that needed attention was an open invoice for a considerable sum of money due from a company called RCA & D.

Herb always laughed about the name of that company. He was probably one of the few people on the planet who knew that there was no R, C, or A at the company but there was a D. Ryan, Cuttler, and Angeline were figments of the imagination of Dugan, the founder, who started a wonderful rumor so that people would think it was a bigger company, more ethnically balanced to please everyone, and it would give Dugan the out to say things like, "I'll have to check with my partners on that," or "I'll take that up with management at the next board meeting." Like its name, nothing about Ryan, Cuttler, Angeline & Dugan was legitimate.

The truth was Dugan was "it!" He was The Man. He was the management and he was the board. The elevator was rigged so that a key was necessary to go to the penthouse where R, C, and A supposedly had their offices. In reality, there was no penthouse, only a panel in the elevator with more numbers than there were floors and a lock into which one could insert a phantom key to go to a non-existent floor.

It always struck Herb as hilarious that everyone fell for that story when all you had to do to know the truth was to stand outside the building, look up, and count the number of floors. Yes, Herb was definitely street-smart.

Herb had things he had to take care of in Colorado so he called his travel agent and asked her to make all the arrangements for him and his current honey. He'd need airplane reservations, a rental car, and a hotel for three nights. That would give him enough time to organize a cleaning service to clean up his new house after the old owner and a painter to put a shine on the place. Then they'd be ready to move in. With a little creative routing, he could be back in New Jersey by Friday night, in time to meet with RCA &D's representative to collect on those unpaid invoices.

Herb left the key to his New Jersey house with the real estate people who promised to find a buyer as fast as possible and Herb took off for Colorado, leaving the telephone number of his hotel in Aspen and the location of his new house just in case they had to send someone to find him to help close a deal on the New Jersey dwelling. Herb knew his cell phone was never reliable in the Colorado Mountains.

Although the realtors told Herb not to expect any miracles, he figured it didn't hurt to be prepared to fly home the same night if needed. After all, it was a great house, in a great location, and he was letting it go well under the market value, at least in his mind.

It was a perfect day. The weather forecast from coast to coast was mild and sunny except for some occasional showers predicted in the southeast. No turbulence was expected in the flight path and Herb was a happy man. He and Florie sat comfortably in first class, drink in hand, enjoying perfect flying weather.

The beautiful weather brought out potential home buyers in droves. Although the realtor knew many of them were sightseers with a fantasy of home ownership and nothing better to do on a gorgeous day, she had no choice but to treat each visitor to the real estate office as a buyer. Who could really tell when fantasy would be motivated by desire and the right price and result in a sale?

Dorothy Lester greeted Leona and Harold Stanton as they entered the real estate office, offered them chairs and proceeded to tactfully delve into their net worth to determine their capability of doing more than wasting her time. The fact that they were house shopping on a Monday made them more viable as buyers than the droves of "lookers" who descended on her office on weekends. Carefully continuing to qualify the new clients with questions to determine if they own a home now, was it sold yet, what was their household income, and, doing her own financial research by checking out the car they drove up in, Dorothy determined, based on the BMW 7 series which they parked outside her window, that these clients could be buyers.

As she reviewed the houses that were available, it became clear that the Stantons had visited almost every other realtor in the area and had seen just about every house listed with multiple-listing services.

"You know," Dorothy began, "We've got an exclusive on a house that's just come on the market. I, personally, haven't seen it yet, but I understand it's beautiful. Let's see," she mused, reading the description, "New kitchen, new bathrooms, multiple fireplaces, swimming pool, redwood decks, professionally landscaped. And I've got a motivated seller, who is on his way at this moment to Colorado to ready his new home for his move. Maybe we should all go over and take a look together. It sounds like it may be just what you're looking for."

Mr. and Mrs. Stanton decided to follow Dorothy in their own car since there didn't seem to be anything else for them to see after this house. They pulled into the driveway and parked in front of the garage doors. They did the normal glancing and scanning of the potential buyer: Mr. Stanton, noticing the neatness of the lawn and paths, and Mrs. Stanton noticing the tiny imperfections. To Dorothy's relief, the key worked and the front door opened easily. The foyer was beautiful. The floor was granite, the walls were marble.

The tone was set for the elegant house that followed. Streetwise Herb Holmes either had great taste or a great decorator. Every detail of the dwelling suggested it walked straight out of Architectural Digest. The place was a palace. The couple was very impressed.

After carefully surveying the living room, dining room, kitchen, den, bedrooms and baths, the realtor led her clients to a stairway, saying, "Let's check out the basement!"

The term basement did not apply. The lower level revealed a mini-arcade complete with pinball machines, a variety of arcade games, a two lane bowling alley complete with AMF equipment, and an antique pool table with electric-blue felt surface.

A side alcove housed a projection room complete with three rows of movie theatre seats capable of seating thirty people. Speakers abounded indicating state of the art equipment. All of the above were included in the price of the house which was, indeed, a bargain, given the appointments of this home.

As they meandered past the parquet dance floor to check out the bar bedecked with soda fountain and draft beer, they noticed what appeared to be a Sub-Zero refrigerator. With Mr. and Mrs. Stanton close at hand, Dorothy opened the shiny chrome door with the same flair she had used in opening the refrigerator in the kitchen and the walk-in closets in the bedroom.

It took only a moment for Mrs. Stanton to see past the cloud that was made by the cold air mixing with the warm room temperature. In another moment, she was out cold on the floor of the basement, her body's protective reaction to the gruesome sight of arms, legs and torso's hanging on hooks in the freezer. Mr. Stanton was on the floor trying to revive his wife as Dorothy flew up the basement stairs as if jet propelled, screaming at the top of her lungs. It took as long to revive Mrs. Stanton as it did for Dorothy to stop screaming.

Supporting his wife as they walked, Harold Stanton arrived in the kitchen and eased his wife into a chair. Dorothy had already called 911. The Stantons saw no reason for them to stay. They had, indeed, seen enough. Dorothy said she would wait for the police to arrive. She had their contact information if there was any reason they were needed. It didn't seem like they should be needed, Mr. Stanton explained, and further asked Dorothy to lose his number.

No sooner had the Stanton's pulled away when the police arrived. They were followed an hour later by the F.B.I. whom the police had summoned. That was followed by interrogating Dorothy and some quick police work that determined the following:

Holmes, who often signed his name "H. Holmes," carries the same name as the first recorded serial killer in the United States, a coincidence that the police could not overlook.

Herb's plane was scheduled to land in Denver where his itinerary indicated he had reserved a car. The F.B.I. prepared its welcome reception in anticipation of Holmes' arrival in Denver.

CHAPTER TWO

HERB AND FLORIE collected their luggage from the baggage carousel in Denver Airport. Pulling their bags from the moving chrome conveyer system, Herb parted the crowd of passengers using his luggage as a shield.

They left the terminal and made their way to their waiting car at the car rental area. Finding their rental car in space number 27, Herb unlocked the doors and, playing the gentleman, held open the passenger door for Florie to get in.

With Florie settled in the car, Herb unlocked the trunk and gave the lid a shove upward. Without focusing on the rising trunk lid, Herb turned away to pick up his luggage. As he turned back toward the trunk to toss the bags in, Herb was shocked by the body in the trunk that lunged up at him, gun focused at his chest.

"F.B.I.! You're under arrest."

Herb dropped the luggage and pivoted in place, instinctively looking for an escape route. To his greater surprise, the car was encircled by a SWAT team of at least twenty men. He knew at once that he was the featured subject of the cross-hairs on the sites of each rifle. This was not a good time to make a move, Herb thought, and sneezing was out of the question.

There was no choice but to surrender and go peacefully while professing his innocence all the way to police headquarters where the F.B.I. would question him and Florie separately.

It was obvious that Florie knew nothing. Her answers were either the result of a good act professing lack of knowledge of Holmes' pastimes, or Florie, indeed, knew nothing of Holmes' endeavors and was possessed by incredible stupidity. After hours of questioning, her interrogators decided that her responses were not an act and Florie was released.

The repeated questioning of Holmes resulted in the same answers. Holmes explained again and again, and again, that he had a legitimate business aiding humanity and that he could account for all body parts which were all legally acquired. He explained that he met all health standards and codes, none of which were of concern to the F.B.I., and that he could prove his legitimacy to them by making a few well placed calls to deans of medical schools, hospital administrators, coroners, and medical examiners in a number of states, all of whom would attest to his ethical practices and legitimacy. He carefully omitted the names of his clients whose direct approach to dealing with unpleasant business issues resulted in a constant flow of inventory to his freezer. A few phone calls to well-titled individuals at respected institutions freed Mr. Holmes with a profuse apology and a chuckle about the additional scare created by the coincidence of his name being that of the first U.S. serial killer.

Herb laughed too, but that was because he was getting the last laugh. How clever he had been to cut off and discard the fingers and heads of the bodies provided to him by sources like RCA & D long before they were recycled into parts. If Holmes hadn't been careful, they'd have nailed him for sure from fingerprints, tattoos, and birthmarks on the body parts.

Being fastidious at his job, Herb overlooked nothing. Like the local butcher, Herb perused each carcass and discarded any unsatisfactory parts either because of their lack of value or the potential for linking him to a crime. It was this attention to detail that made Herb the man of choice for such jobs. And while the police scoured above the earth and under stadiums for missing mobsters, Herb enjoyed his private knowledge of their noble end in the name of humanity and research.

You just can't be too careful, Herb thought to himself as he exited the police station and walked toward Florie who was sitting on a bench outside, bewildered by the extraordinary events of the day. Refusing the offer of a ride from the F.B.I., Herb hailed a taxi and instructed the driver to take him to the nearest car rental location.

Let's try this again," Herb laughed, happy to have beat the system and convinced more than ever that a mountain retreat was the answer to his future needs. It was time to live a simple life. And if things didn't work out with Florie, he could always get her recycled by one of his remaining contacts.

Never burn all your bridges, Herb thought as the taxi made its way to a new era in his life.

CHAPTER THREE

IT WAS THE perfect Sunday in June that everyone had prayed for. The soft breeze carried the perfume of the blossoms and the trees and the sun glistened on the rows of white ribbons, flowers and bows that lined the walk. Soon the guests would arrive and join the two families assembled there to witness the marriage of their children, Maisy and Frank.

It seemed like only yesterday that they watched Maisy graduate from high school. It seemed like only yesterday these same family members and friends attended Maisy's graduation party. The irony was that it **was** only yesterday.

Maisy's parents had insisted that Maisy graduate from high school before she and Frank married and, to meet the letter of the law they had set down for her, Maisy planned her wedding for the day after graduation. What a weekend!

As the guests arrived, it was clear that they were beginning to grow weary of the rounds of rituals and celebrations being heaped on Maisy in one compressed weekend and the demands placed on them to exude their joy while suppressing their impulses to indulge in the kind of gossip one would expect from the timing of the two events. Who could blame them from pandering in rumors that Maisy was pregnant and that this must be the proverbial shotgun wedding?

The rumors seemed all the more believable when you looked at the couple. They were so mismatched. Maisy was still very much the giddy, scatterbrained teenager, frequently described as flighty. She was fun to be around but completely focused on nail polish and hair rinses. Her husband-to-be, six years her senior, was tall, olive-skinned, and dark haired and made quite a contrast to Maisy's pale skin and auburn hair. It didn't take much to figure out that it wasn't Maisy's mind that interested Frank. But it was difficult to see how someone as cute as Maisy, with a flair for making people feel comfortable and keeping them laughing from her antics, could find anything about Frank to love other than the attention he showered on her.

Frank could best be described as devoid of personality. No one could remember ever seeing Frank smile. The contrast of bouncy, bubbly, buxom Maisy and dull and dour Frank added to the undercurrent of buzzing of the guests and propelled the rolling of eyes among those trying their best not to speak ill of this moment of joy.

The sad part about the rumor was that it was not true. But it would take nine months before the gossipers figured that out.

Maisy's parents walked a fine line between wishing she would postpone this wedding, grow up, meet a warm, friendly person that the family could truly embrace and hoping that their sensual teen seductress would get married before the gossip that filled the air became true. Nonetheless, everyone nodded accordingly, smiled cordially, and agreed that this was a marriage made in heaven, while wishing both families all of life's blessings.

While the guests filled the seats of the sanctuary of Temple Shalom Lev, many tried to rise above the temptation to focus on the negative by chatting about items they read in "Newsday," the Long Island newspaper of choice. Of course, the topic always came back to the same place: "Did you see Maisy's picture with the graduating class . . . right next to the announcement of her wedding?" You just could not escape it. It was too much to resist.

Hilda and Nathan Goldman had done their best to provide a loving, caring, and protective environment for Maisy to grow up in but she was a "Wild Thing" with a body that made heads turn. And Frank's head was no exception. Unlike the Goldman family, Frank's folks just never quite made it to the better part of town. While the Goldmans were "comfortable," the Mandells struggled by with the bare necessities which added to the, "What could she possibly see in him?" rumor-mill.

The flowers in the sanctuary mixed with the perfumes and designer aftershaves of the guests. Melanie Cohen's head turned as the aroma of Santos de Cartier encircled her. Passing her aisle seat was a six-foot living display straight out of "Gentleman's Quarterly."

"Who's he?" she asked a temple member seated to her right.

"That's David King. He's chairman of the Ritual Committee. He'll give the bride and groom Sabbath candleholders as a gift from the congregation as part of the wedding ceremony," the elder temple board member replied. "He gets to come to all the Baby Naming ceremonies, Bar and Bat Mitzvahs and weddings to present gifts to those celebrating on behalf of the congregation. He's a legitimate gate crasher!"

"He's the kind of guy you like to look at . . . and he smells good, too," Melanie added.

"He ought to look good. He comes from big money. His family owns the land this temple is built on and they built the temple for the congregation. They lease the temple to the congregation for one dollar a year," the elder continued, beaming with a sense of pride in knowing righteous people.

"It's nice to know there's somebody out there with money who actually knows what to do with it, "Melanie chimed in. "Looks like he knows how to do more than just keep himself in threads."

Not everyone among the assembled represented wealth. Many came from hard working backgrounds and were there to celebrate Nate's joyous occasion. There were more than a dozen men sitting in the temple who not only respected and admired Nate, but who owed their lives to him. During his career of over thirty years in the Nassau County Police Department, Nate had saved the lives of these now retired police officers and firefighters. These people idolized Nate for his selfless heroism. There wasn't anything they wouldn't do for him.

Melanie, too, was devoted to her Uncle Nate who was her mother's favorite brother. Melanie had wonderful memories of afternoons at Aunt Hilda and Uncle Nate's house. There was always a badminton net set up in the backyard from Spring through October, and year round, their house was full of games in progress like Scrabble, Clue, Monopoly, and jigsaw puzzles growing with each of her visits. The smell of Aunt Hilda's wonderful southern specialties cooking in her kitchen, like fried tomatoes and sweet corn, met guests at the front door.

Hilda grew up barely south of the Mason-Dixon Line. Although she had lived on Long Island since her marriage to Nate, she exuded southern hospitality and thought of herself as a Southern Belle.

Sitting in the temple in anticipation of Maisy's entrance brought so many childhood memories rushing into Melanie's thoughts. She remembered summer drives to Jones Beach with Nate, Hilda and Maisy and jumping the waves holding Uncle Nate's hand while Maisy mirrored that image on Nate's other side. Melanie's memories were so vivid she could almost smell the cocoa butter aroma of the suntan oil Aunt Hilda swabbed on her back and shoulders and the fresh smell of the salt air that enveloped the beach.

How strange it was that so many buried memories rose to her consciousness pushing out the whispers and excitement of the moment.

CHAPTER FOUR

AS MELANIE STUDIED the beauty of the stained glass, the sculptured doors of the Holy Ark, the warmth of the richly carved wood of the pews, she, too, was caught by the contrast, not of the bride and groom, but of the permanent display of plastic plants that lined the altar. A long, narrow wooden flowerbox ran along the edge of the top step of the altar and was filled with plastic greenery. The bouquets, and giant vases filled with sprays of white roses and Baby's Breath distracted the eye from the dusty, tacky, "practical" plastic display that obviously acted as "decor" when live flowers were not provided by a family celebrating a special event.

Melanie's creative senses were already envisioning a quick redecoration.

"All it would take is to toss out those tacky green things," Melanie thought, "and put vases filled with live flowers inside the planter each week. What a difference that would make. And how much could it cost?"

Melanie had been a temple member for a long time but she was never very active in temple business or politics. She enjoyed services and adored the rabbi but she was so uninvolved that she had never realized who David King was or the incredible contribution he and his family made to the community. Melanie decided it was time she did something too. Finding a way to get rid of the plastic eyesore from this otherwise spiritually motivating environment seemed like a good thing to do. She'd have to make time to follow up on that.

The sound of a crescendo of "Ah-h-hs" drew Melanie's attention away from her thoughts of improving the sanctuary to the unquestionably most delectable item, Melanie's cousin. Maisy had just entered from the double doors at the back of the sanctuary accompanied by Hilda and Nate. While Maisy beamed like the sun outside, tears filled Hilda's eyes and Nate looked like he was walking the last mile. The mixed messages were quite clear. The truly caring could only hope that Maisy's state of mind would last forever while the gossipmongers anxiously awaited the emergence of the next rumor.

For the moment, there was only one truth: Maisy was radiant and had never been happier. That was the theme of the day even down to the band at their reception playing, "Who Could Ask for Anything More?

Melanie wondered if she would ever find someone who would make her feel that there was a missing piece that was needed to complete here life. So far, there was no "perfect fit" and she preferred to be uncompromisingly independent. For Melanie, single wasn't scary. Married to the wrong man, however, was a thought she found terrifying.

The wedding, the reception, the bride's gown, the flowers were as beautiful as they could possibly have been. Hilda saw to that. Maisy was her only daughter and she was going to give her the right send-off regardless of the fact that she was convinced that she was sending Maisy off to the wrong man.

By tradition, the honeymoon plans and their payment are the groom's responsibility. For that reason, the honeymoon consisted of one night in a motel off of the New Jersey Turnpike and an afternoon at the slot machines in Atlantic City. Maisy had barely removed her wedding gown and the honeymoon was over. Actually, it was worse than over. Because Frank was in a pitifully low-paying job, an apartment of their own was out of the question. So the honeymoon ended with Frank carrying two nylon duffle bags across the threshold of Hilda and Nate's house while Maisy brought up the rear carrying the large garment bag that housed her wedding gown. This was not the romantic beginning to their life together that Maisy would have liked. Maisy's sense of reality heightened as she and Frank entered her teenager's bedroom, their new home together. As Maisy looked around at the underwear she had left on the floor just hours before their wedding, the open bottle of nail polish still on the night table, and every cosmetic, toiletry, deodorant, and hairbrush known to mankind on her dresser, Frank surveyed the room for one square foot of uncluttered space to put down the two nylon duffle bags. Not finding a spot was the defining moment of the newlywed's first fight. It started so simply with Frank's words: "Do you have to be such a slob?" to which Maisy responded by bursting into tears and running to the kitchen in search of Mommy and Daddy.

As she burst into the kitchen in a state of emotional distress, Nate turned to Hilda and said, "And they said it wouldn't last."

CHAPTER FIVE

IT WAS SUMMER. It was hot, muggy, humid and steamy, and that was just the climate in Maisy and Frank's bedroom. Outside wasn't much different. For the newlyweds, the sex was good but not as quiet as Nate and Hilda would have liked.

Every morning, Frank got up, got dressed, went out to the front porch to fetch the morning newspaper, grabbed a cup of coffee and sat at the kitchen table silently as he drank it and drank in the front page of The New York Times. Hilda reached over, removed the crossword puzzle and became engrossed in solving it. When it became clear that Frank was not going to speak first, Hilda offered a cheery,

"Good morning." Frank could not bring himself to partake in this simple, civilized exchange.

"What's the matter, Frank?" Hilda asked. "Can't you say 'Good morning?'"

"I don't like mornings," he replied, hardly moving his lips in the process.

"Well, I'm not crazy about mornings, either," Hilda responded, her uncombed hair and wrinkled housecoat attesting to her statement. "But that doesn't stop me from wishing you a 'good morning'," in a voice Frank described as "Southern Tokyo Rose."

There was no reply from Frank who drank his coffee silently as testimony to his lack of interest in participating in any morning rituals. As Frank walked wordlessly out the front door to go to work, Hilda turned away and mumbled, "Maybe he gives at the office."

At eleven o'clock in the morning, Maisy rolled over and opened one eye as if testing to see if it was worth her time to crawl out of bed. She put on a plush terry cloth bathrobe, walked into the bath room and, after taking care of her most basic needs, put her toothbrush in her mouth and emerged from the bathroom. As she meandered into the kitchen with her toothbrush dangling from her mouth, she found Hilda sitting at the crumb-covered kitchen table, her hair still uncombed. The only evidence to the outside observer that any progress had been made on this day is that Hilda had finished the NY Times crossword puzzle and had dragged the day-old copy of Newsday from a kitchen chair to the table to catch up on the local news.

"Good morning, Mommy."

"Good morning, Baby Girl."

For the next hour, the scene was frozen as Maisy sat transfixed, toothbrush dangling from her mouth, wading through Newsday's social section, comics, and clothing ads, removing the toothbrush from her lips only for occasional sips of coffee.

This became the daily household routine.

CHAPTER SIX

BY THE TIME Frank came home at six o'clock, Maisy was dressed in pink stretch pants that took on a second-skin quality, she had pulled the quilt over the rumpled sheets, Hilda had dressed and combed her hair, and the kitchen was ready to receive the foursome for dinner. Maisy, playing the loving wife, ran to the door to greet Frank.

"Hello, Honey. Did you have a good day?" Maisy asked. It was a scene modeled after, "I Love Lucy."

The grunt-like sound that Frank emitted could not be interpreted.

"Hi, Frank," Hilda yelled from the kitchen. "Go get ready for dinner. We'll eat dinner as soon as Nate gets home."

Now that Nate was retired, he visited with retired friends, dropped in at the Senior Center, and volunteered at community organizations. He kept busy every day, leaving in the morning for his workday of civic activities and playing cards, and tried to come home for dinner about the same time every night, often bringing with him fresh fruit and pastries that he picked up in his travels or pieces of wood from the lumber yard that he might use in his next project.

Hilda stuck her head out of the kitchen into the living room to see if Frank heard her since she got no response. Frank was already halfway up the steps of the split-level house on his way to the bathroom. It was obvious that he had heard Hilda and just as obvious that communication was not Frank's best thing.

This night, Nate arrived home with bundles and boxes from the bakery. He was a tall man, well over six feet. Few men in his age group were that height physically. It was the rare man who was his height spiritually. Nate had an all-knowing calmness about him that demonstrated the depth of his wisdom. It was clear that he wasn't a genius. He was a simple, humble, easy-goin', genuine nice guy with solid common sense, good street smarts and a reputation as the kind of guy who would give you the shirt off his back. Everyone agreed he was the perfect match for Hilda who professed to love him dearly.

Nate unpacked the fresh rolls and cakes he had brought home from the bakery as Maisy and Frank settled into the cramped corner where the round table was lodged. As he sat down, Nate said," So, how was your day at work, Frank?"

"OK," Frank responded.

"So, how is the auto parts business these days?" Nate continued, trying to draw Frank into the family dinner conversation.

"OK," Frank replied.

"You sell much today?"

"Some."

"You don't smile much, do you Frank?" Hilda chimed in.

"I smile at work," he answered.

"I suspected that," Nate said with a chuckle.

"What's that supposed to mean?" Frank asked.

"I just mean you've got a handsome face and it would be nice to see you smile once in a while, that's all," Nate explained.

"Look, all day long I have to smile at customers. When I come home I don't have to smile and I don't want to smile," Frank declared.

"Leave Frank alone, Mama," Maisy jumped in.

"Why don't we all just eat our dinner before it gets cold," Nate, the peacemaker, suggested. "I bought sticky buns for dessert!" Nate announced, trying to adjust the mood. What he missed was that it would take a surgeon to remove Frank's personality to change the mood.

As they were finishing dinner, the lack of conversation was interrupted by the telephone ringing. Nate answered the phone. It was his favorite niece, Melanie, checking in to see how everyone was doing, as she did almost weekly or as the need presented itself, and to tell Nate and Hilda, once again, what a beautiful wedding it was.

"Yes," Nate replied. "Too bad you can't bottle those kinds of days. It would make a helluva product!"

CHAPTER SEVEN

THE SUMMER PASSED with incredibly monotonous routine. Frank and Maisy engaged in passionate and noisy sex nightly. Frank awoke early, had his coffee silently, earned his reputation as a cold, unfriendly grump, and came home in the same state, with fatigue as the only additional feature, to be met by sexy Maisy who finally relieved herself of her dangling toothbrush in the late afternoon giving herself just enough time to be dressed by six p.m.

Dinner conversation was carried by Nate and Hilda, Maisy still playing the child's role, while Frank acted as if he were a truck who pulled into their kitchen, as if it were a gas station, just to tank up.

Had Hilda been asked, she would have agreed that Frank was about as communicative as a truck.

Maybe it was the change from hot and humid to crisp and brisk that September ushers in that brought the change in Frank. One night at dinner, Frank stunned Hilda and Nate by saying a full sentence that wasn't related to passing food on the table.

"I'm thinking about changing jobs," Frank muttered.

"You are? You didn't say anything to me about that," Maisy pouted.

"Well, I'm saying it now," Frank shot back.

"What are you thinking about doing?" Nate asked.

"I've got this account I've been sellin' auto parts to and they like me," Frank went on. "They asked me to come over and talk about a job."

"Well, what do they want you to do?" Nate asked

"Similar stuff to what I'm doing over at the auto parts place . . . sales, bookkeeping, customer service."

"You must be fabulous at customer service," Hilda remarked, sarcastically.

"I'm damn good at my job," Frank shot back defensively.

"What kind of company is it?" Nate asked.

"It's an investment banking firm," Frank answered. "They have a fleet of cars for their executives and they've been buying parts through me for a while now."

"That's the most I've ever heard from his mouth at one time," Hilda thought, a smile spreading across her face at the idea.

"Well, what do you know about investment banking?" Nate asked.

"Don't ask him like that, Daddy. Frank's plenty smart," Maisy whined.

"I took courses in high school and I took some more accounting courses in night school. They said they were impressed by my customer service skills and my accounting knowledge. And they say they'll train me and teach me the rest." Frank delivered the last line like an attorney resting his case.

"What kind of money are they offering you, Frank?" Nate continued to probe.

"Twice what I'm makin' now!"

"Twice?" Nate asked, incredulously.

"Actually, a little more than twice! They say they'll start me at $55,000 and there's more to come if I learn well and do my job the way they want it done. Maisy and I will be able to move out of here and get an apartment of our own and live on Easy Street," Frank concluded.

"There's no such place, Frank," Nate cautioned.

There was a silent period around the table as each of them let Frank's announcement sink in. Frank seemed to have run out of steam from the monologue he had just delivered

"Well, who is this company?" Nate queried.

"Ryan, Cuttler, Angeline, and Dugan," Frank said proudly.

"Oh, no you don't!" Nate exhorted.

CHAPTER EIGHT

"WAIT A MINUTE, Nate!" Frank shot back. "Who the hell are you to tell me what I can do and can't do? This is my ticket out of here. This is my chance for success. I think you're just jealous 'cause you didn't make that kind of money at my age."

""Nate doesn't have a jealous bone in his body," Hilda retorted, protectively. "You watch your mouth and you take that back, Frank."

Nate turned to Hilda, proud of her defense of him, and asked her to take Maisy for a walk so he and Frank could talk alone. Hilda and Maisy dutifully complied and, then, Nate continued.

"Listen, Frank. Those guys are bad people. They've got a bad reputation. If they get their hands on you, you'll never get out from their clutches. Don't fall for the easy money," Nate concluded.

"It's not easy money. I'm going to be working a lot of hours doing important stuff," Frank defended.

"Frank, think about what I'm saying to you," Nate went on. "You're responsible for Maisy, too. I'm telling you, Frank, these people are no good! Stay away from them! No one's been able to make anything stick, but they're a shady organization. Don't do it, Frank!"

As he said these words, Nate stood up, pushed his chair away from the table and walked out of the room. Frank muttered, "He can't tell me what to do," and then lapsed into his customary silence, which went unnoticed since Frank sat alone in the room.

The next morning, Frank came down earlier than usual. It was obvious at once that he had taken extra steps in grooming himself. His hair was slicked back, his tie was in a Windsor knot, his shoes were glossy, his nails were spotless, and all of the items he was wearing coordinated. The final touch was that he smelled of sweet spices. This was a man with an agenda. And his agenda had given him confidence and altered his mood with the intoxication of the excitement that the day would bring.

Frank sauntered into the kitchen. He swaggered over to the coffeepot and poured himself a full mug. He turned with the flair of a man on top of the world and said with gusto, "Good Morning, Hilda," to which she responded,

"Good grief, what's come over you?"

"Boy, you sure can't win around here, can you?" he replied.

"That's all right," he continued. "I'm a rising star, in charge of my own destiny. You'll see," he said with finality. "You'll see."

As Frank walked liltingly down the front path to his rusting car, Nate appeared on the sidewalk and said, "Don't be a fool, Frank. These people are no good. Stay away from them! You're gonna get yourself in trouble. I know what I'm talking about!" Nate's thirty years on the police force made that statement good as gold.

Nate's final words of warning were lost on Frank as the noisy rumblings of his muffler drowned the words of reason and wisdom that he was offered.

CHAPTER NINE

MARBLE AND BRASS were seen in abundance on the outside and inside of the building. Over the entrance were the bold, brass letters: R C A & D. He was home. He could feel it in his bones. This was the best thing that ever happened to him. He was one lucky guy. $55,000 . . . and that was to start. He and Maisy could tell them all to go to hell now. What did they know, anyway, the jealous bastards.

Frank surveyed his image in the floor-to-ceiling mirrors surrounding the elevators. "Lookin' good," he told himself.

"This is one swell place," he thought as he stepped around a huge urn filled with long-stemmed fresh flowers centered on an inlaid marble table. The classical music playing in the lobby and the elevator convinced him of the "high-brow" sophisticated nature of one and all who worked in the building.

Fitting in here was his aspiration. Frank wasn't going to continue the trend as a "poor Mandell." People were going to be jealous of him for a change. They want to gossip? They want to spread rumors? He'd give them plenty to talk about. He always knew that living well was the best revenge.

And today would be the beginning of his beginning.

As he stepped out of the elevator onto the executive floor, Frank thought, "I'm going to leave the old me in this elevator and enter my new life here as a different man."

Frank was right about that.

Frank approached the receptionist with an uncharacteristically confident and dazzling smile. The receptionist asked him to take a seat, pointing to the plush, upholstered wingback chairs, while she let Mr. Dugan know he was here for his 9:30 appointment. Frank used the time to memorize the waiting area : lush hunter green velvet upholstered chairs and loveseats seemed to float on glossy pearl gray marble floors; richly textured tapestries hung from large brass rods; exotic fresh flowers abounded in huge Chinese vases; tabletops of colored inlaid marble were everywhere. What Frank would have liked while he waited there was a Coke, but a soda machine didn't appear to fit in with the decor.

Frank pretended to immerse himself in Business Week but he just couldn't get into the articles. He looked around for a newspaper but didn't see one. He decided it had to be wherever the soda machine was!

Three hours later, the receptionist called his name and gave him directions to Mr. Dugan's office.

When Frank entered Dugan's office, he noticed the imposing grandfather clock and was surprised to note the time was 9:40.

"Well! Frank, my boy! Welcome, welcome, welcome. I'm so glad you could make it today. How about some coffee?"

"No, thank you. Thank you for the opportunity, Mr. Dugan. You've got quite a place here."

"We're not complaining. So let's talk about you. Are you ready to tackle a career at Ryan, Cuttler, Angeline, and Dugan?"

"Yes, sir, I sure am! I hope I can do all the things you want me to do."

"Nonsense, my boy! We see by the quality and quantity of things that you juggle over at the auto parts place that you are a versatile young man. And, frankly, no pun intended, we only look for three things, Frank. They are: a brain that can understand exactly what we ask you to do; a predisposition to being loyal; and the ability to be completely honest in your relationship with our organization. We figure that everything else you can learn but those things are in you or they're not. In other words, we expect you to do what you're directed to do, be completely and devotedly loyal to us, and never to lie to us, cheat us, or steal from us. Now that shouldn't be difficult to do for a fine young man like yourself, eh?"

"No, sir," Frank replied enthusiastically, smelling money in the air and power on the horizon.

"All right, then, my boy," the rotund, gray-suited Dugan chortled, "before we show you to your office and get you started in your new career, we have a little traditional induction ceremony that we go through to welcome new members to our investment group to drive home our welcome message and clarify those three things we look for in a memorable way. Sort of like the scouts' court of honor or a priest's ordination, you know. Now hold on a second here while I buzz . . ."

Dugan's voice trailed off as he reached for the button on his intercom and shifted his attention to organizing the official welcoming for Frank.

While Dugan instructed his secretary to send a senior executive to his office to accompany Frank to his Welcome Ceremony, Frank's mind danced with the ease and wonder of it all.

"I'll have my own office in this beautiful building. I wonder if I'll get my own secretary. Boy, what tradition. I wonder if I'll get a company

lapel pin at the welcoming. Boy, would I like to flaunt that. I'll never take it off. I wonder if you get a signing bonus at the ceremony. Stay calm, Frank. You'll know any second now."

Frank's thoughts came to an abrupt halt as the door opened and a tall, slender, well dressed man came in and introduced himself. "Hello, Frank! Welcome aboard! I'm Jason Edwards, Vice President of Consumer Services. Charles tells me

I'm the lucky one who gets to escort you to your welcome ceremony. I'm delighted! Why don't you come with me then and we can get started. See you, Charles."

"Yes, do drop in after you get Frank all settled in," Dugan responded. "I've got a number of things I need to review with you."

Frank graciously and enthusiastically thanked Dugan for the fantastic opportunity and promised Dugan he'd never regret hiring him and that he'd never let Dugan or the company down. Dugan made appropriate noises in response and the door closed behind Frank and Jason leaving them in the wide, high-ceilinged hallway.

Frank was delirious with joy. For the observer, that would go unnoticed for, on the outside, his demeanor was controlled and placid. For Frank, this was not an act.

As he walked down the corridor, Frank drank in his surroundings. Grey marble rose from the floor halfway up the wall where it was met by hunter green fabric that continued to the ceiling. The contrast of color, cold against warmth, hardness against lush, served to reinforce Dugan's welcoming address. Pictures of the Colonial Fathers, The Hunt, and The First Thanksgiving abounded, neatly framed in rounded brass. A large brass hunting horn hung next to an original painting of the RCA&D building which was signed by the artist and dated 1893. Clearly, dignity, propriety, and professionalism exuded from every crevice of the place. What could Nate have been thinking when he carried on about this company. *Jealousy does strange things to people, Frank thought.*

The corridor turned left and continued on endlessly with more of the same except that the wall covering above the marble changed to a hunter green and burgundy plaid. It reminded Frank of a blanket he had as a child. This was truly an omen that he had done the right thing, made the right move. What was there really to think about anyway?

Who could pass up that salary and the good life it would bring. *I'm the man, now, Frank thought. This must be Heaven.*

Jason had been babbling on cordially all the while, pointing out offices of sales, marketing, accounting and administrative people all of whom had spacious lushly carpeted offices with mahogany desks and green glass covered brass desk lamps. The best offices were occupied by the investment advisors. Jason explained that they met with clients in their offices and so they all had floor-to-ceiling windows, comfortable sitting areas with sofas, club chairs and coffee tables with sterling silver coffee services on them, and round mahogany conference tables with high back wing chairs. The gray, green, and burgundy color scheme abounded with individual offices taking on two of the three colors in solids, plaids and stripes. Overall, it was a Ralph Lauren dream.

Finally, after a walk that can only be compared to walking to your departure gate at Dallas-Fort Worth airport, they came to a side corridor and made a left turn as Jason, droning on about the square footage and history of this prestigious building, slowed his pace and finally stopped in front of a solid white shadow-panel door. It was massive, easily four and half feet wide, eight feet high and adorned with large decorative brass hinges and colonial style brass doorknob. There were no other markings to distinguish the door, but it was clearly the entrance to the rest of Frank's life.

He held his breath as Jason reached out and inserted the key. What exciting ritual would he find behind this door, Frank thought. His mind raced through a collage of candles, stained glass, incense, signing his name, no, no, scratching his name into a two hundred year old table along with the names of people who worked in this building long before RCA & D owned it; melting wax and making a seal next to his name in a huge handmade book that was the size of a standard office desk; using the company seal to mark the spot of the entry of his name and his start-date as key executives and staff, assembled for this moment, applauded. All of this and more raced through Frank's mind in the nanno-second that it took Jason to turn the doorknob.

"Welcome to RCA& D, Frank. You have a home and a future here," Jason said with sincerity and passion. "We expect big things from you. As you enter our company, we want you to reflect on the difficulties and obstacles of your past, the promise of your future, and the words Mr. Dugan shared with you about what is important to us at RCA & D. You will have some time for quiet reflection as you prepare yourself to meet the challenges we will face together on our company team. Take all the time you need. There's no rush When you're done, just head home, get a good night's rest and come in at eight-thirty tomorrow morning ready to conquer the world. And don't be late now. Promptness and daily attendance are important parts of that commitment to the company that we expect from you, Frank."

Jason had concluded his little speech. Frank was riveted in Jason's gaze. He felt like he was that little boy at Boys Town who was uplifted by the attention, support and caring of a saintly priest. He really fell in this time, he thought. He finally got a break. His ship had come in.

Jason positioned Frank at the edge of the door opening. As the giant door opened, Jason's arm on Frank's back gently nudged him inside. With one swift, firm movement, Frank was whisked across the threshold and could feel the closing door on his back.

The room was pitch-dark. Frank's eyes could not adjust to the darkness. He could not tell how big the room was or where a step in any direction would take him. He felt a sense of panic set in and bit his lip to keep from calling out. *Keep calm*, is all that came to his mind. *Keep calm and don't move.*

First, he tried to find the doorknob, sliding his hands up, down, and side to side over the door. There was no doorknob. Pushing on the door did not open it. Clearly, it was locked from the outside.

"Why am I in here?" Frank's mind raced.

He wasn't sure he felt any sensation in his legs but his arms seemed to be working. Extending both arms, he put his palms out reaching across the walls trying to determine the size of the space he was in. His weight shifted and he lost his balance for a moment. His right foot pivoted trying to recapture his balance. He heard the scratching sound of grit and dirt grind under his feet. There was no plush carpet on this floor.

Frank's mind raced as he tried to make sense out of what was going on. His breathing quickened. His heartbeat raced. Panic was taking over. He was trapped, he was alone, he was in a black hole. How did he get here? And how would he get out? Were they taping his reactions on infrared film? Was this a test to see how well he would do in unusual situations? Stay calm, he thought. Stay cool. Don't lose it now.

Afraid to take a step, he stood in place, arms clinging to the walls, back against the door. It seemed like he passed through the doorway hours ago when only minutes had passed. He wasn't sure if his voice would work. Maybe Jason didn't realize that the lights weren't on. That was it. How silly. "Jason," he called. "There are no lights on in here," Frank said, trying to sound casual through tight vocal chords.

"Jason," he repeated, banging on the door with the palms of his hands, not daring to turn or move.

There was no response.

What now.

Think, Frank. Use that head of yours, is all that raced through Frank's mind.

Finally, he came up with a plan. He would slide around the edges of the room, clinging to the walls with outstretched palms, blindly scanning the room for a light switch. Slowly, he extended his right leg sideways, bringing his left leg to meet the new destination once his footing was established. Repeating this dance of darkness, Frank glided like a butterfly in two-step motions, arms fluttering up and down the wall.

As he moved from left to right, Frank could hear the dirt beneath his feet grind. Grit from a rising mound created by his left foot rose and dropped over the top of his shoe, running down into his shoe and creating another discomfort in an already miserable situation. Dust created from his darkroom gavot began to fill the air. Frank could taste the dirt and began to sneeze from the unseen cloud forming in the stale air.

Frank moved around the first wall to the corner, then another corner, and finally reached the door again, never finding a light switch. What now? Dizziness ensued. Panic welled within him. Banging on the door was the only solution.

As he turned and faced the door with his raised fists, the room took on a glow. Frank turned again, hugging the door with the palms of his hands and facing the center of the room. He looked up at the ceiling at the source of the glow as his eyes began to readjust to take in his surroundings. At the top of the ten foot ceiling was a single, bare light bulb. It couldn't have been more than 20 watts,

Frank thought. For a room with a ceiling this high, it did little more than define the space.

As Frank's eyes adjusted to the dim light, he saw that the walls were painted, not the decorative gray, green and burgundy he had enjoyed earlier, but black.

The light cast a strange glow and was absorbed by the black walls in the windowless room. The room looked to Frank to be square in shape and about nine feet in each direction.

The floor of the room was completely covered with dirt. Frank took his already filthy shoe and pushed some of the dirt aside to find the flooring underneath. There was just too much dirt and no sub-flooring to be found. Frank's eyes moved slowly from his focus on his shoes in a straight line along the floor to the middle of the small room. He saw what appeared to be the wooden legs of a carpenter's sawhorse, the kind of wooden structure they use to control crowds at parades. There was one on each end of the room. Frank inhaled deeply and gasped in the silence as the vision in front of him registered in his mind. There, balanced on the sawhorses, was a six and half foot long open coffin.

Morbidly, Frank stepped closer for a better look. On the white satin pillow lay a card with bold, large letters. In the dim light, Frank strained to read the one word message: VACANCY.

CHAPTER TEN

HEARING A CLICK, Frank tried pushing the door again. This time it gave way and, having burst out of the black room, Frank exited the building by the stairway at the end of the small hallway. Frank raced down the eight flights of stairs skipping two, sometimes three, at a time. Running breathlessly, his heart thumping, Frank knew he was living a nightmare he had awakened from so many times since childhood. The stairs and walls were painted institutional gray and the flights were separated by cage-like chain-link dividing walls. The sensations of flying and falling mixed together as Frank made his way at breakneck speed downward through the building.

When he emerged on the street and felt the cool air touch his body, Frank felt a chill rustle through him. At first he thought it was an emotional reaction. Then, he realized that he was soaking wet. Sweat poured from his skin and urine drenched his trousers. He was wet, cold, and beginning to mildew. He was not a pretty sight. But even the soothing shower he took when he got home did not calm Frank nor did it remove the stench he felt clinging to his body.

The corner seat at the kitchen table took on special meaning for Frank. It was comforting to feel the two walls behind him meet at the center of his back giving him some sense of security. He sat there, coffee cup in hand, with a dazed, distant expression on his face.

He was startled by Nate's entrance. One glance at Frank confirmed for Nate that Frank was shaken by something.

Geez, man, you look like you got hit by a truck," Nate remarked, reacting to the disheveled and disoriented aura surrounding Frank.

Frank was a vision of gray, taut skin and unkempt hair from running his fingers repeatedly across the top of his head in an unconscious effort to release the stress and relieve the pain created by today's events.

"Snap out of it, fella. I'm talking to you," Nate continued. "What's the matter?"

"Oh, God," is all that came from Frank's mouth. A low groaning sound again carried the words, "Oh, God." Frank held his face and head cradled in the palms of his hands, elbows resting on the kitchen table. He had managed to keep it all together until this moment, but Nate's show of concern brought him back to his toddler years when he would suffer a scraped knee while the babysitter was there, but not run crying about it until hours later when his mother returned home from her job at the tailor shop.

"What's the matter, man?" Nate asked again.

The terror on Frank's face frightened Nate, a man who had survived two wars and thirty years on the police force. He knew that look. He had seen it on the countless faces of men returning from combat without their buddies, without their limbs, without their spirit. It was a look that Nate had hoped he would never see again. What could have happened to Frank to plunge him into such a desperate state, Nate wondered.

"Talk to me, Frank," Nate implored. "What happened?"

Frank relived the day for Nate. While the trauma of the experience embraced and shook Frank, Nate listened attentively showing neither emotion nor shock.

Frank knew Nate well. He was a warm, caring, sensitive man. Frank knew he could rely on Nate to understand. This was the second shocking surprise for Frank this day. When Frank completed his tale, Nate asked coldly, "What did you expect, Frank?"

Frank stared at Nate blankly. "What do you mean?"

"I told you these people are bad, Frank."

"I know. I believe you," Frank answered, staring fixedly at the table, afraid to look into Nate's eyes." But what do I do now?"

"What do you mean, 'What do I do now?'" Nate asked, using a whining mimicking tone.

"What do I do, Nate? How do I get out of this? I don't want to work for these guys!"

"Now is not the time to ask that question. The way out was not to get in!" Nate bellowed. "So congratulations. Don't you get it, Frank? You're in. All the way in!

They own you. And the only way out is in that pine box. So take your new found wealth and get the hell out of my house."

Nate stood up with his last words with such force that the wrought iron framed chair he had been sitting on tumbled over. Leaving it on the floor as if to punctuate his remarks, Nate made for the archway to the living room. Framed in the center of the arch, Nate turned and glared at Frank whose eyes were now fixed on Nate.

"But understand one thing well: You keep Maisy out of everything, ya hear? If they touch a hair on her head, I'll shoot you dead with my service revolver."

Nate walked out of the kitchen, promising himself never to tell Hilda the details of Frank and Maisy's exile. It was the last time Frank would be seen looking for security in Nate and Hilda's kitchen between the cornering kitchen walls.

When Maisy returned from her nail salon appointment, Frank was half packed.

CHAPTER ELEVEN

MELANIE COHEN AWOKE with a mission. She showered and dressed quickly, eager to catch the rabbi at Temple Shalom Lev during his morning office hours. It was time for her to perform her mitzvah, her good deed, for the congregation. Melanie jumped behind the wheel of her car with enthusiasm. She was exhilarated by the thought of the blessing she would bestow by bringing the beauty of fresh flowers to the bema, the temple's altar, replacing the dusty plastic greenery. It is unfortunate that she did not remember the lessons of history so concisely expressed by Clair Booth Luce: No good deed will go unpunished.

As she entered the temple, there was a flurry of activity in the foyer. It was Friday morning. So much had to be done by the committee appointed by the Sisterhood to prepare for the arrival of the Sabbath at sunset.

A peek into Rabbi Ezra Levy's office quickly revealed that he was in the building but not there. His eyeglasses lay across a huge pile of papers and his keys were next to his desk phone. Melanie pivoted on her heels and retreated down the hall.

Following the sounds of chatter, laughter and clanking dishes and silver, Melanie entered the area where the Oneg Shabbat would take place after services. Tables were set with coffee urns and festive platters of cookies. Sliced cakes wrapped in colorful cellophane and ribbons adorned the tables. A focal table displayed a jumbo challah, the braided ceremonial bread, and bottles of wine surrounded by tiny waxed paper cups barely larger than thimbles. Beautiful bouquets of flowers decorated the tables around the room, provided by the family whose daughter would celebrate her Bat Mitzvah this weekend.

Melanie recognized one of the women standing near the coffee urn and approached her. Melanie knew more about her than she realized.

Her name was Allison Shapiro. She was tall, thin, very attractive, in her mid-twenties and the mother of two children under three. Her husband was taller, older, handsomer than most and an all-around great guy. They lived in a beautiful, well decorated, and immaculate home. Allison was a wonderful mother, a great homemaker, and a terrific wife who made time to devote to the temple.

It was a pleasure to see Allison and her husband, Dave, at temple functions, celebrations, and holiday festivals with the children. What a beautiful family. And what lovely people they were. There was no question that God had smiled on this union. They were the perfect couple.

"Hi, Mel," Allison called across the room. "I haven't seen you since Purim. How have you been?"

"Terrific," Melanie responded. "I almost didn't recognize you without your Queen Esther costume! How are the little ones?" she asked, having forgotten their names.

The two women spent the appropriate two minutes in idle chit-chat before Melanie asked her question. "I' m looking for Rabbi Levy. Have you seen him?'

"Who's looking for me?" a voice boomed from across the room.

Melanie twirled around to face the rotund figure coming toward her.

"Rabbi! I'm so happy I found you!'

"Correction! I found you," he chuckled, his whole body enjoying his joke. Nowhere could the joy of the Sabbath be reflected more than on the face of Rabbi Levy. He radiated the spirit of peace and joy and personified the traditions of more than five thousand years of Sabbath celebrations. But while he embraced ideals, ethics, and universal truths, he was a bottom-line man with no tolerance for bullshit. This made him a controversial figure because he rarely concerned himself with being politically correct and consumed himself with his focus on "morally right and just." The result was that Rabbi Levy was either adored or disliked. There was no middle ground.

Melanie was firmly entrenched on the "adoring" side of the rabbi. She found that her social relationships with temple members were with those who held the rabbi in the same esteem with the same fervor. While there were those who criticized every comment and every move the rabbi made, in Melanie's eyes he could do no wrong. If there were saints in Judaism, she would have placed Rabbi Levy's name in nomination. And not that he was a saint. Not by a long shot. But the things he did for people and the way in which he did them qualified him to be counted as a Righteous Man. At least in her eyes.

The rabbi embraced Melanie with an overenthusiastic bear hug, squeezing the air from her lungs. "It's so good to see you. Have you joined the Oneg Shabbat committee?" he asked.

"No, rabbi," Melanie responded, wanting to end that conversation before she became entrapped by one more commitment of her time.

"Well, you're certainly welcome," Allison interrupted. "We can use all the help we can get. And I think you'd enjoy it. We actually have a lot of fun!"

Melanie did her best to smile while trying to ignore the recruitment efforts.

"I have an idea, rabbi, and I thought I should talk with you about it," Melanie began. Turning her back on the work of the committee members, most of whom had withdrawn to the temple kitchen.

"What's on your mind, Melanie?"

"Take a walk into the sanctuary with me, Rabbi. I'd like to show you something," Melanie began.

The rabbi walked with Melanie, his hand held behind his back, exuding the aire of a Biblical sage. Melanie explained her idea of replacing the artificial plants that lined the raised platform of the *bema* with vases of fresh flowers and potted plants, that she would purchase, have them delivered, and dropped in place weekly for which she would pick up the cost.

The rabbi listened thoughtfully, without expression while Melanie spoke. Although she knew he was listening, Melanie could not devine his reaction until she said what seemed to be the magic words:" . . . and for the High Holy Days, we could have fresh white flowers across the whole bema in keeping with the tradition of the white robes you, the cantor and the choir wear to reflect the purity of the holiday," she concluded.

The rabbi's eyes sparkled. His entire face lit up. His smile was so full that his eyes seemed to disappear. And inside Melanie, there was a joyous delight elevating her by the rabbi's appreciation of her idea and the gift she wished to bestow.

"This is great," he said. "Just great. What you need to do is talk to David King, the Ritual Committee Chairman. It's a wonderful plan but it has to be approved by the committee and David is a good place to start. Come into my office, Mel, and I'll give you his business and home phone numbers. Go catch up with him and make it happen," he instructed. "It's a wonderful idea!"

They hugged, then parted. Melanie bounced toward the temple doorway, almost making it through when she heard her name echo off the marble floors.

"Melanie, wait!" It was Allison Shapiro again. She drew close to Melanie who stayed in place, her right hand on one of the huge cast-bronze entry doors.

"Listen, Mel," she began. Melanie hated sentences that began that way. They were usually followed by words she did not want to hear. "We've got a great team of women who volunteer to help get everything ready for the after-services celebration each week. Sometimes a sick child or some other minor emergency leaves us shorthanded. Can we count on you to pitch in and help us out from time to time?"

Melanie's lack of enthusiasm and fear of trespass on her time must have been obvious by the look on her face and her pose of paralysis to which Allison quickly responded, "I'm not asking you to make a permanent commitment. I'd just like to be able to give you a call if we run into a jam."

How could you refuse a harmless request like that? Probably just by saying "no," Melanie thought. And even *she* was surprised as she heard herself say, "Sure."

Melanie kicked herself all the way through the parking lot. How did she let herself get caught in that one! The last thing she wanted to do was set buffet tables for hundreds of people. You better go home and practice saying, "NO'" in the mirror one hundred times, she told herself.

Melanie started the car's engine, making a promise to herself to call David King the second she got home. As she waited for the light to change, Melanie's enthusiasm overtook her and she decided to pull off the road to call King's office to see if he was in. Maybe a quick drop-in would get some attention and get the ball rolling.

Melanie called King's office. When the receptionist answered, she asked to speak to David King.

"I'm sorry but Mr. King is out of town until next Wednesday. May I take a message?" the receptionist asked.

"No message. I'll call again," Melanie answered. "Why was nothing easy?" she thought.

CHAPTER TWELVE

FRANK AND MAISY moved into a motel while they looked for an apartment. All their worldly goods fit into the trunk and backseat of Frank's rusty car and consisted mostly of clothes, Maisy's cosmetics and magazine collection, souvenirs and photos recording her life with Frank. The entire lot was not worth more than twenty dollars at a garage sale. But this was their fortune.

On the drive from Nate and Hilda's home to the motel, Frank decided that the first thing he would do when he got his first paycheck would be to go out and buy himself a new car. Well, maybe not a brand new car. Just a car that was new for him and newer than the twelve year old clunker he was driving.

While Frank spent his days at RCA & D, Maisy was out looking for a place for them to live. Maisy's cousin was in real estate and offered to pick her up and run around town with her looking at potential apartments and houses for rent. At least that will keep her days occupied, Frank thought. Although he looked forward to getting out of the motel and into a place of their own, Frank knew he couldn't allow himself to get distracted by this chaotic beginning of his married life.

Frank tried to focus on learning his new job, whatever that meant. He tried to block out the memory of the black room but it was his first thought every morning and his last memory as he fell asleep at night. The rest of the time, he made every effort to shut the experience out of his mind.

So far, Frank had done little in his new job except rearrange some books on the shelf in his office and read mail that was addressed to Occupant. He looked forward to being given some kind of specific assignment, not because he wanted to prove his value, but out of sheer boredom. No one called him. No one asked for him.

He wasn't really sure at this point why they hired him. On the other hand, if they were willing to pay him for doing absolutely nothing, he would find a way to keep himself busy and keep a low profile.

Each day for the last two weeks, Frank had arrived at eight-thirty in the morning as ordered by Jason. Since then, he hadn't seen Jason once. Maybe he was out of town. On his first day, Frank was shown by the receptionist to his small but very attractive office. As he entered and hung up his jacket, the receptionist told him that he would be called when they were ready for him. Frank assumed that would be in a matter of minutes or hours and decided to use the time to make himself feel at home. In ten business days, no one had sent for him.

When Frank finished drinking his morning coffee and reading the Occupant mail, he opened the newspaper to the sports section to check on his teams. There wasn't anything else to do anyway. The loud buzz on his intercom startled him. It was a new sound in his office.

"Frank, it's Dugan. Would you mind stepping into my office for a minute?"

Frank pushed every button on his telephone until he found the one that allowed him to reply, "Right away, sir."

Frank slid into his jacket and left his office, buttoning the jacket as he walked briskly down the hallway. It seemed so long ago that he was here being welcomed into the company by Dugan.

Dugan smiled warmly at Frank and pointed to a plaid wingback chair for him to sit in. Frank nervously crossed and uncrossed his legs, finally opting to sit leaning forward with his elbows on his knees and his fingers laced together.

"Frank, there's a little bit of business I want you to take care of for me. There's a fellow we do business with from time to time. He performs a great service to the world of medical science. What he does is provide hospitals and medical schools with body parts that they use in their teaching seminars to train new doctors and to keep physicians up-to-date with current surgical techniques. We have a contribution to make to his inventory and I need you to connect with him so he can arrange for pickup. At the same time, I thought we would kill two birds with one stone," Dugan continued. He must have caught the change of expression on Frank's face with his last sentence and quickly added, "Let me clarify that for you. You are going to meet the President of Mr. Bodyparts in Atlantic City. All of the information as to where and what time tomorrow night you will meet is on this paper. You are going to give him this envelope which will provide him with location information for our contribution to his company's fine work."

Frank reached out and accepted the itinerary and the sealed envelope without looking at them.

"Now the second item I was referring to directly refers to you, Frank," Dugan continued.

Frank's heart skipped a beat.

"You've been here two weeks and it's pay day. Here's how we are going to take care of that. You've got a nice young wife and, being newlyweds, we thought you'd both enjoy the chance to have some fun. So this is how pay day is handled for you. After you deliver the envelope to Mr. Bodyparts, go to the crap table in the casino of that hotel. Get control of the dice and, when you win, take your winnings to the cashier. Don't worry about how much you win at the table. It will be properly adjusted at the cashiers' window. Take your money and leave the casino at once. You and your bride are already checked in at the hotel for one night with our compliments. So go enjoy dinner, a show, sleep late in the morning, take a walk on the boardwalk, and drive home at your leisure." Dugan stopped speaking. Frank was afraid to ask anything but he did have one logistical problem carrying out the plan.

"Mr. Dugan, I've got a slight problem," Frank began timidly.

"What's that?"

"I don't think my car can handle a trip to Atlantic City and back. It's in pretty bad shape. I'm thinking about buying a new one."

"I hope you don't mind our planning ahead on this one. We noticed your car in the employee lot and we agree that your vehicle is not sturdy enough for the trip, and that it is not in keeping with the image of RCA & D. Makes us look like we don't take good care of our employees. And if there's one thing we know how to do, it's how to take care of people," Dugan concluded. The irony was not lost on Frank. "When you leave today, you'll find a suitable vehicle in your parking spot. The keys are on your desk in your office along with the registration and insurance card. I hope you find it to your liking." It was clear that Dugan's presentation had come to an end and that all that was left was for Frank to say the appropriate exit lines and leave.

Frank called Maisy from his office to tell her they were going to Atlantic City for the weekend and she should pack enough for one night and the next day. Maisy was thrilled by Frank's spontaneity and thought he was the most romantic man in the world.

Frank picked up the keys, the car registration and insurance papers and the papers Dugan had given him. Realizing his pockets weren't adequate to hold all of the items, Frank determined that the time had come for him to invest in a briefcase.

The silver Cadillac parked in Frank's space completely suppressed any thoughts Frank might have had about meeting a man whose company deals in human body parts. Frank had already internalized that he was dealing with the devil. The most he could hope for was that he could reap the benefits without being caught up in the middle of something horrible. After all, he was just a customer service rep with some night school bookkeeping accounting courses. What could he possibly be asked to do besides shuffle some papers, record some numbers, and deliver some documents?

How simply Frank had rationalized everything! He was just a pencil-pushing delivery service.

Sheer joy embraced Frank as he peeled out in his silver Cadillac humming the tune they played at his wedding reception, "Who could ask for anything more?"

CHAPTER THIRTEEN

FRANK'S ELATION OVER his new possession overshadowed any doubt that things would be great if he just kept his own nose clean and did what he was told. His whole life he did what he was told, Frank thought, and for the first time it was paying off. Now was not a good time to grow a conscience.

Frank wasn't the only one with good news. Maisy had found a great apartment for them that she was so sure he would love that she signed a lease. The rent wasn't too bad and she was so happy about it that Frank figured it didn't pay to explain to her why she should have waited for him before she locked them into anything. It was only a one year lease, Maisy said, and there were other serious renters according to her cousin, the realtor. Since she got Frank's message that they'd be away for the weekend, she figured she had better pounce on it before the trip or it might not be there on Monday.

Grabbing their bags, Frank led Maisy out to their new car. "Their" new car was something of a misnomer. Actually, according to the registration, it was RCA & D's new car, but why quibble? For his purposes, this was his car.

They made their way southward along the New Jersey Turnpike to the off roads and followed the signs to the Jersey shore. Traffic was unusually light for a weekend but that was probably because of how early they got on the road. Frank had left the office right after Dugan gave him the assignment and Maisy had taken the apartment early in the day which cut short any other housing shopping that was on the realtor's agenda.

When they arrived at the hotel, Frank presented himself at the front desk. The treatment he received elevated his sense of self-importance. Maisy was so proud to be with Frank as the hotel staff fluttered around like a member of royalty was checking in.

A bellman escorted them and their duffle bags to an oceanfront suite. Maisy decided that she would pretend this was the honeymoon suite she had fantasized.

"This place is big enough to land a plane in," Frank mumbled.

"Oh, Frank, you're so witty!" Maisy bubbled, still trying to flirt with her husband to keep him interested in her charms. If Frank could be described as anything associated with wit, it would have been nitwit, but Maisy wasn't smart enough to notice that.

Maisy decided to take a bubble bath in the huge sunken tub in the bathroom. Frank thought that was a great idea since it would give him a chance to do the job he was sent here to do. Leaving the sound of running water behind him, Frank took the papers he was given and headed to the lobby. He made a mental note of stopping in a leather goods shop and buying a briefcase and luggage befitting a classy guy like himself. *Image* was the new important focus of his waking hours. He shouldn't be seen getting out of his Cadillac with his papers in his hand and his clothing in nylon zippered sacks.

Frank's concerns about connecting with Mr. Bodyparts and finding his fortune at the crap tables evaporated as he crossed the lobby. He turned as he heard his name called from a nearby sofa. A man walked toward him, put out his hand and said, "Good to see you, Frank. I've been waiting for you. The front desk buzzed my room when you checked in," the man continued as if talking to an old friend.

Frank was overwhelmed. Was this the right person? Should he just give him the papers and go back to his room? Should he invite the guy for a drink?

While this was Frank's first experience as a courier, it was not this stranger's first time receiving documents from a stranger. Frank had no choice but to follow his lead.

"Frank, you've got an envelope for me, no?

"Yes."

"This is the part when you give it to me," the man answered.

"How do I know you're the right guy?"

"Who else knows why you're here?"

"Nobody."

"Exactly my point! Papers please," he said, handing Frank a magazine. "The less conversation, the better."

The man told Frank to take the magazine, sit down on the sofa and skim through it, then place the papers in the magazine. He'd be nearby. When Frank put the magazine and its treasure on the coffee table, he'd come over and pick it up. He instructed Frank to look for him in the lobby in the future and use the same procedure for all future communication.

Frank followed directions carefully and, in less than three minutes, the transfer was completed.

One down, one-to-go.

Frank walked into the casino and went to the first crap table he saw. After watching and making small bets for ten minutes, the dice were his. He bet twenty dollars and won. He bet another twenty and won. This couldn't be luck. How did they know who it was? How were they able to make him a winner? Wasn't that what he wanted his whole life, to have somebody make him a winner? RCA & D had his eternal loyalty. They didn't need to use the scare tactics. A car and a fancy hotel suite were enough to own him.

He had a pile of chips in front of him. He had no idea how much he had won in the last five minutes. He began to feel swept away with the power of winning, completely forgetting that chance had nothing to do with his success.

He bet fifty dollars and, to his great surprise, lost for the first time since he stepped up to the table. It was clear that that was his cue to quit.

Frank scooped his chips into a waxed pint sized cup and headed to the cashier.

As he started away from the table, he remembered to put his hand in his pocket and find a twenty dollar bill to tip the croupier.

At the cashier's window, he pushed his pot of chips through the glass cage. A man came up behind the cashier, tapped him on the shoulder and whispered something in his ear. The cashier slid off his stool and disappeared through a doorway into the back of the house. The man took Frank's chips, dumped them into a counting machine and counted out money for Frank. There was no correlation between the value of the chips and the money Frank was given. The money was neatly placed inside an envelope and pushed through the cashier's window.

It was no surprise to Frank that the amount of money he received was equal to two weeks' pay. The nice part was that there were no deductions. This was a sweeter deal than Frank imagined. At no time did the consequences of his actions enter Frank's mind. This was Easy Street. He'd heard about it. Now he lived on it. Life was good.

Frank took his winnings to the front desk. It seemed like a good idea to put the cash in the hotel safe or a guest safe-deposit box. It didn't occur to the untraveled Frank that there was a safe in his suite. As he approached the reception area, there was Mr. Bodyparts checking out. Frank overheard the desk clerk wishing him a safe trip home and inviting "Mr. Holmes" to come back again soon. Herb Holmes turned his attention to the bellman and away from the front desk in one movement. He never saw Frank approaching nor was he aware that Frank now knew his name.

Removing one hundred dollars from the envelope and placing it in his wallet, Frank gave the envelope to the clerk, signed a piece of paper, and was given a canvas sack with a lock on it into which he placed his new found treasure. Frank headed for the elevator to the tower suites patting his jacket pocket that held the little key. He and Maisy were going to have a great time tonight.

CHAPTER FOURTEEN

FRANK RETURNED TO the office on Monday with a renewed sense of himself as a great man on the rise. He had found the "cushy" job of his dreams. The money was good and the perks were even better. Maisy had taken him to see the new apartment on Sunday and, for the first time ever, he actually thought she had used good judgment jumping on the place. Maybe she wasn't so dumb, after all, he thought. It was a great little place with terrific views of gardens, a big pond, and graceful weeping willow trees. It was a peaceful place. Most of the tenants were newlyweds or older people so there were no children to be seen or heard. A definite plus, Frank thought.

Frank gave Maisy a wad of cash and told her to go buy things for the apartment.

Maisy drove Frank to the office, took the car and headed to the nearest coffee shop. It was much too early to go shopping, and besides, she was hungry. Frank was in too much of a rush to get to the office so Maisy was left to have breakfast alone.

After she ordered her eggs, toast, and coffee, she reached into her purse for her cell phone. She decided she needed company for her little shopping spree. She wanted someone to share her excitement, share her decision-making and, from force of habit, share the expenses of the day.

She called her cousin, Susan. Susan was only two years younger than Maisy but a light year more mature and academically gifted. Although the two of them enjoyed each other's company and both shared a crazy sense of humor, in general, Maisy was a kind and giving soul and Susan was a self-centered tight-ass. Maisy always wound up feeling taken advantage of after a visit with Susan. Susan always felt she had spent her time with a moron after a visit with Maisy. Nonetheless, it did not stop them from getting together again with the expectation that they would have a great time. Maisy had already decided that she would get what she wanted from this day. She would have Susan's company, benefit from Susan's opinions of the items she considered buying, and, today, she would take advantage of Susan to get even for prior injustices. Maisy had renewed self-confidence that came from being Mrs. Frank Mandell and the driver of a brand new silver Cadillac.

When Maisy reached Susan, she announced her news about the new apartment. Susan already knew that Maisy and Frank had been ejected from the Garden of Nate and Hilda. News travels quickly in a tightly knit family. News also gets embroidered. Of course, no one knew the real reason for their move but that would not stop the rumors and lies from growing and being embellished. Those who thought Maisy was pregnant at her wedding were sure they moved to have room for the baby that *must* be on the way. Others were convinced that two women could not share one kitchen. Of course, those people didn't know either of them very well or they would have known that one kitchen was one too many for their needs. Nate would never tell anyone the real story. Never! Not even Hilda. It would scare her to death. It was not Nate's style to retell the story. No value in doing that at all and he had no wish to be associated in any way with the realities of the circumstances that Frank brought into his home.

No, Susan only knew they had moved out. And who could blame them. The rumor that Susan had heard was that Maisy's teenage bedroom in Hilda's split level was no place for a newlywed couple. So it all made perfect sense! What did not make perfect sense was for Maisy, who was already in the shopping area, to drive all the way to Susan's house so they could turn around and drive back to the mall. Besides, Susan was taking advanced placement courses at Hofstra University for gifted high school students and had far too much work to do today. She was up to her eyeteeth, she tried to explain to Maisy, in research and papers she had to write and deadlines she had to face, to do anything as frivolous as go shopping with Maisy.

Maisy would hear none of Susan's explanations or excuses. She begged, whined, and enumerated every favor she had done for Susan since they were toddlers including listing every blind date she had ever arranged for Susan and all the places she had chauffeured her since she had a driver's license and Susan did not.

The last argument was irrefutable. Susan caved in and told Maisy to give her an hour to get ready. She would have to pull an all-nighter to get her work done but she did owe Maisy something. And since she wouldn't have her driver's license for at least another year, this would not be a good time to piss off her chauffeur. Maisy had been really good about getting Susan around Long Island. And Long Island was not a place you wanted to be without a car.

Maisy was delighted. She ate her breakfast slowly, enjoying the pleasure of the moment created by manipulating Susan. And she was supposed to be the dumb one. People used ridiculous tests to measure intelligence, Maisy thought. They really should use real life situations. That's the only part that matters, she concluded, completely satisfied with herself.

Maisy picked Susan up exactly one hour later. Susan was all ready to go. Susan had an athletic look about her. Her hair was cropped short like a swimmer or serious tennis player. She preferred man-tailored shirts and chinos. Even as a child, she shied away from frills and laces and party dresses, preferring more practical clothes that didn't hinder her while climbing trees and rock piles.

As teenagers, while Maisy was struggling to walk in high heels, Susan's idea of dressing up was wearing clean sneakers with neatly folded over sox.

To this day, Maisy and Susan were polar extremes on every level. But they were cousins. And they shared a common bond of birthday parties and family celebrations, holidays and tragedies, and the network of gossip and stories that surrounded all those people they referred to as "family."

Maisy found a parking space next to the entrance to Macy's in the Roosevelt Field Mall. She turned off the engine, turned to Susan and said, "That'll be two dollars."

Susan looked at Maisy, startled by her request. "What?" she asked.

"I said, 'That will be two dollars.'"

"You're kidding," Susan responded.

"No, I'm not."

"What for?" Susan asked in amazement.

"For gas," Maisy answered.

"For gas? Are you out of your mind?"

"No."

"Well, I beg to differ with you. You are a cottin' pickin' nut job, Maisy! Where do you get off asking me for gas money?"

"Well, it's just the right thing to do when somebody takes you somewhere in their car, that's all," Maisy explained.

"What are you talking about? I didn't even want to come here today. I wanted to stay home and do my schoolwork. You dragged me out on this expedition. Where the hell do you come off asking me to pay for gas?"

Maisy opened her mouth to continue her explanation of why her request was just and proper but, before she could get one word out of her mouth, Susan had bolted from the car and, reaching for her cell phone as she made her way across the parking lot, was in search of a prime intersection where she could be easily spotted when her mother came to pick her up. Her mother would never believe this one. There was no doubt that this incident would not only result in two cousins not speaking for months but also in two aunts not speaking, as well, as a result of the ensuing "Do you know what your daughter did to my daughter" conversation that would follow.

Maisy was forced to shop alone and make her own decisions about colors of towels and sizes of pillows while Susan walked to the agreed corner of Old Country and Glen Cove Roads to wait for her mother to pick her up. It was a trying day for each of them.

CHAPTER FIFTEEN

WEDNESDAY COULD NOT come fast enough for Melanie. While she busied herself with other things, she just could not get her mind off the happy look on the rabbi's face when she told him of her idea for the flowers on the bema. David King would be back in his office today and Melanie was determined to get to see him or nail him down for an appointment to discuss her plan. But she had her own business to attend to today in Manhattan and would make a project out of reaching David King in between her own agenda.

Melanie showered, dressed and drove to the Long Island Railroad station. She caught up on her sleep on the long train ride to New York City. She arrived hungry and with no time to stop for breakfast so she decided to pick up a muffin and orange juice at a "take out" shop in Penn Station to eat on the run on her way uptown.

The lines at the food shops were long but, spotting one that seemed a little shorter than the rest, Melanie took her place at the end. She looked around at the signs, the shops, the people, with no particular resting point for her gaze.

While standing there, she became aware of the good looking young executive standing in line in front of her. He wore a beautifully tailored suit under a navy blue cashmere top coat and carried a leather attaché case with brass trim. His shoes were polished to a high gloss finish. He was a picture of rising success straight out of "Black Enterprise" magazine. He appeared to be about twenty-eight years old. Standing next to him was an older black man, probably about sixty-five years old. He was wearing a plaid jacket and brown trousers. Melanie thought they might be father and son. She theorized that the father was a blue-collar worker, maybe employed in Penn Station, who had put this young man through college, maybe even law school, and now they met in the morning for take-out breakfast to share together before they each went their separate ways for the day.

But as Melanie continued to watch, she noticed that the older man did all the talking and the younger man stood still and stared straight ahead, not acknowledging the older man at all. She strained to hear the old man talking but, with the noise in Penn Station, she could not catch full sentences.

Everyone took a few steps forward as the line moved up closer to the take-out window. The young man kept his attention rigidly forward and made no moves to make eye contact with the older man. Finally, it dawned on Melanie that the old man was panhandling. The next few words she heard sounded like the older man was saying that he was hungry. The young executive continued to ignore him.

Melanie could stand it no longer. Tapping the young executive on the shoulder, she asked, "Excuse me, sir. Is this man with you?"

She, too, got no answer. She asked again, this time eliciting the response, "No."

"Is he hungry?" she asked.

When she received no answer from the young man, she turned to the older man and asked, "Are you hungry?"

At this point, the line had moved up and the young executive was placing his order at the window. Melanie turned to the older man and addressed her question to him.

"Are you hungry, sir?"

"Yes, ma'am, I am."

"What do you want to eat?" Melanie asked as the young executive stepped away with his brown sack and they stepped up to the window. The older man looked stunned.

"Tell the man what you would like to eat," she said, pointing at the server behind the glass window. As he began to point at the array of pre-made sandwiches and speak, the counter clerk, waving his arms wildly at the black man, bellowed," Get out of here! We don't want your kind around here! Get lost!"

"Sir! Sir!" Melanie exploded at the counter clerk. "This man is my guest," she continued as she turned to the older man and said," Please tell the man what you'd like."

"Can I have an egg and cheese sandwich?"

""Give my guest an egg and cheese sandwich, please," Melanie told the counterman.

"Would it be okay if I had two? I haven't eaten in three days," the older man continued.

"Give my guest two sandwiches, please," Melanie told the clerk.

"Thank you, ma'am. But could I get another one for the lady in the corner across the station. She hasn't eaten in days either. There are so many hungry people around here."

Melanie opened her handbag and searched for her wallet. When she found it, she discovered she had only $25 in cash. Removing it from her wallet, she handed the bills over to the clerk.

"Here's $25.00," she said, "Wrap up as many sandwiches as that will buy."

The clerk obeyed and set about loading the food into brown sacks. The older man began thanking and blessing Melanie profusely, much to Melanie's embarrassment.

When the limit of the money's purchasing power was reached, the clerk handed Melanie the brown sacks. Melanie and her breakfast guest stepped off the line and stood facing one another as Melanie handed him the bundles of food.

"Oh, thank you, thank you, ma'am and God bless you."

"Don't thank me," Melanie replied. "It's not necessary. But I am giving you this food with one condition. You must GIVE it to people who are hungry and you must not sell it."

"Oh, no, ma'am. I'll give it to the hungry. Don't you worry about that. I'll watch over these bags of food," he said.

"And who is going to keep you honest and watch you?" Melanie asked.

"The Good Lord is watching me, ma'am," the homeless man responded.

As Melanie started to move away, the man reached into his pocket and then held his hand out to her. Melanie extended her hand to see what he was giving her. The man placed a shiny item in her palm. Melanie brought her hand closer to her tear-filled eyes to see what it was. Upon closer inspection, Melanie's eyes brought into focus a quarter.

A simple quarter.

A quarter that represented all the worldly wealth that stood between the hungry man and zero net worth.

Melanie gasped. "Oh, no" she said. "I can't take this. No, no."

"Please let me pay you what I can," the man responded.

"Oh, dear God, no. You keep it. Please. Please give out the food while it's still hot."

Melanie turned and sped out of Penn Station, tears flooding her eyes. She realized she was doing just fine while she was buying the food to take care of the man and the unmet hungry strangers in Penn Station. It was his gesture of offering her his last quarter that pushed Melanie's emotions over the edge. She knew she would never forget that encounter.

Melanie stopped at an ATM machine to get some cash and then hopped in a taxi to go uptown to her meeting. It took longer to get to the meeting than it took for her attorney to review the papers Melanie needed to sign on behalf of the family's foundation and her trust fund.

When she arrived, her attorney, who had been the family's legal counsel for over 30 years, greeted Melanie as she entered the meeting room. Clemont Marvin Goldman, or C. Martin Goldman as he liked to be called, had known Melanie since she was a child. One look at her told him that something was wrong.

"Melanie, are you all right?" Clement asked.

"I was in Penn Station, and . . ." was all that Melanie could say before she burst into tears.

"What's the matter? Are you hurt?" Clemont asked, worriedly. "Take off your coat. Let me look at you. Turn around!" he said as he examined her physical condition.

"Well, you're not injured. What is wrong, my dear?"

"In Penn Station . . ." was all that Melanie could say. She sat on the sofa in Clemont's office and cried for the next two hours.

It took Melanie six months before she was able to retell the story of the events in Penn Station, but she still cried when she reached the part about the quarter. And she always wondered how the nice looking, well groomed, young black executive could have just stood in that line like a totem pole and ignored a hungry man.

With family matters in order, Melanie checked off the visit to C. Martin's office and moved on to the next items on her TO DO list. She called her favorite NYC hair salon and got an appointment for a haircut which would require her to stay overnight in the city unless she wanted to fight the rush hour to get home. Next, as inconsequential as those plastic flowers in the sanctuary were as compared to the homelessness and hunger that abounded around her, Melanie decided to focus elsewhere to lift her spirits and forced herself to place a call to David King's office in hopes of getting that appointment she wanted to speak with the man, himself. Her optimism was dampened by learning that he was on a call and couldn't speak with her now. Perhaps she would like to leave a message.

"No, I'll call again," she said.

And again. And again. And again.

And each time she learned that David King was on a call.

"Well, I'm a call, too," she said, indignantly, to the receptionist.

Seeing the humor in Melanie's remark, the receptionist chuckled and said, "Let me see what I can do for you. You must have something pretty important to talk about. What is this, your tenth try today?"

"Something like that," Melanie said, relieved that the receptionist was a sweet lady and not the defensive type who would have given her a speech about it being King's first day back and what a busy man he is and who are you anyway?

A moment later, a deep voice came on the phone and said, "This is David."

Having succeeded in step one of her mission, Melanie was shocked into momentary silence.

"Hello? Is anybody there?" David asked.

"Yes. Yes, I'm here. I was just so stunned that I actually got you on the phone. I've been waiting to talk with you since last Friday and I've tried to get you a dozen times today, so I'm just thrilled that I actually got through to you," Melanie blurted out in one breathless statement.

"Well, I'm glad for you too. But may I ask who are you?"

What a dunce you are, Melanie thought, now feeling self-conscious and uncomposed.

"This is Melanie Cohen. I'm a member of Temple Shalom Lev, too. I've spoken to Rabbi Levy about an idea I have for the temple and he suggested I speak to you as the Chairman of the Ritual Committee. Do you think you could make ten or fifteen minutes for me to explain my idea to you?" Melanie held her breath waiting for his answer, half expecting him to say he's much too important a person to be bothered with the likes of her and her idea.

"Well, I've just gotten back from a little business trip and that puts me at a disadvantage trying to catch up with everything around here. Today is already Wednesday so this week is shot. Next week is over-programmed as it is." He paused a moment and then said, "Tell you what. How is a next Tuesday? Will that work for you?"

"Sure. What time?"

"How is eleven-thirty in the morning?"

"That would be perfect, Mr. King."

"My name is David," he replied.

"Thank you, David. I look forward to seeing you then."

Melanie ended the call and enjoyed the excitement of her first triumphant step. And David King sounded like a terrific guy. This was going to be easier than she thought. But then why shouldn't it be? Who could argue with beautiful flowers that she would pay for?

Melanie circled that agreed upon Tuesday on her calendar and wrote in the time and his name, last name first. It stuck her as funny that her calendar now read that she had an appointment with King David.

CHAPTER SIXTEEN

AT 8:00 AM Friday morning, Melanie was awakened by the telephone ringing on her night table. Fumbling with her eyes closed, she found the receiver and brought it to her ear with a thump.

"Ouch, hello," she moaned.

"Melanie, it's Allison Shapiro."

"What time is it?" Melanie strained to ask.

"Oh, Mel, did I wake you?"

"No, I had to get up to answer the phone. It was ringing," Melanie answered, incoherently.

"Melanie, we need you," Allison continued, ignoring Melanie's attempt at humor.

"Who is *we*?"

"The Friday Morning Committee! Esther's daughter is sick and Sylvia broke her arm. It's down to me and Old Mrs. Benjamin. I *need* you, Melanie. Please come and help. I've called everybody else on my list and so far no luck. You are my last hope."

It was clear that Allison was begging. Melanie wished she had just asked her. The begging was humiliating. At this hour of the day, it was more than Melanie could deal with. She wished she had the strength to say no. She'd have to practice for next time.

Melanie dressed quickly to take on the day with her usual intensity. The sooner she got there, the quicker they'd get done, she thought. She raced through the bathroom and bedroom completing her morning routine, poured a glass of orange juice for herself in the kitchen, and whirled through the foyer to the garage to jump into her car.

As she drove her car through the streets of her private community, she noticed a cluster of neighbors talking animatedly on the corner where the school bus stopped. Mostly, she noticed there were no children present. Clearly, the school bus had come and gone and what was left was a gathering of adults flailing arms, a sea of red faces, and voices loud enough to be heard through the closed windows of her car.

Melanie slowed down and stopped at the corner. She opened the car window, leaned over the passenger seat to get closer to the assemblage and yelled, cheerily," Hey, there! What's up?"

"Have you got a minute, Melanie? I think you need to know about what's going on here," Agnes Palermo urged.

The tone of her voice derailed Melanie's immediate schedule. Something of importance was obviously afoot. Melanie turned off the engine, got out of the car, and joined the sidewalk group.

"So, what's up? Is the electric company planning to put a nuclear reactor in the neighborhood?" Melanie asked.

"No," Agnes answered. "Worse!"

"What could be worse?" Melanie asked, naively.

Agnes came right to the point.

"We're taking up a petition and we need everyone in the neighborhood to sign it."

"A petition for what?" Melanie asked.

"Not FOR! Against!' Agnes continued.

"Against what?" Melanie responded, wishing Agnes would get to the point.

"Against the impending sale of a house around the corner to an undesirable element," Agnes exploded to the background sounds of what appeared to be nodding sheep.

"Are underworld figures moving in?" Melanie asked incredulously.

"Underworld?" Agnes repeated, quizzically. "No! They're blacks. BLACKS! And we won't have it," Agnes pronounced each word emphatically. "That's why we're getting up a petition."

"Sounds more like a *posse* than a petition," Melanie responded. "Well, have a great day, everybody," Melanie yelled as she smiled broadly and moved toward her car. "See y'all soon."

"Well, we can count on your support, now, can't we, Melanie?" Agnes called after her.

Melanie stopped, pivoted on her heels and looked back at the group.

"W-el-l," Melanie drawled out. "I just don't know how my grandmother would feel about that, Agnes. She was black, you know."

Melanie turned back toward her car and smiled broadly as she imagined the looks on the faces in the crowd.

"Well, I'll be damned," Agnes said. "Who would've thought that!"

Once inside her car, speeding away, Melanie burst into laughter. "Stops 'em in their tracks every time," she giggled to herself, imagining the group wondering if they should take her at her word, imagining the older neighbors saying things like, "I knew Melanie's grandmothers on both sides. They sure didn't look black. But who knows? Maybe one of them 'passed.'" "She imagined her grandmothers having a good laugh from the grave. Melanie's sense of humor and sense of honor came from someplace. She was sure they were both having a proud moment in Heaven today.

Then her thoughts turned to the group. "Hypocrites!" she thought. "Agnes the Hypocrite! Sainted Agnes the Hypocrite!" As Melanie's mind raced, she realized that she was also racing through town streets. She concentrated more on driving but couldn't keep the scene on the corner from intruding into her mind.

How strange it was that Agnes, the self appointed neighborhood spokesperson rallying anti-neighbor sentiment, was the same Agnes who held Sunday School classes in the family room of her home because the church didn't have enough classroom space to accommodate all the children.

The same Agnes who gave catechism classes in her home every Wednesday afternoon, every year, from September through May. The same Agnes who volunteered to go to the rectory three days each week to cook dinner and act as housekeeper to help keep church expenses down. The same Agnes who was leading an inquisition against some unknown family. Hard to believe.

When Melanie arrived at the temple shortly after 9 AM, she saw Allison busy setting a buffet table. The woman helping her was Old Mrs. Benjamin. Melanie was sure that "Mrs." was her middle name because everyone referred to her as Old Mrs. Benjamin. Melanie had to stop and think before addressing her directly.

Melanie didn't mind helping but she really wasn't into this. She wanted to make it clear that calling her for this purpose was not to become a habit.

"You know, Allison, I'm usually not around on a regular basis," Melanie began. "I have meetings and appointments that take me into

Manhattan quite frequently. Several times a year, I go into the city and stay there for two or three weeks at a time because I have to be there everyday and the commute is a killer. So I just stay in until all my business is completed," Melanie concluded. "I want you to know because if you call and I'm not there for days or weeks at a time or if I don't return your call, it may be that I'm just not around." Melanie had now established the basis for dodging invitations to play on this committee. But the fact of the matter was that it was all true.

"That's okay, Mel," Allison responded. "I'm just thrilled you're here today."

"What do you do that takes you to hotels in the city so much?" Old Mrs. Benjamin creaked. Melanie could feel the threads of gossip that weave into the tapestry of rumors beginning to form on Old Mrs. Benjamin's words.

Melanie didn't feel like explaining her life at this early hour of the morning to this old biddy. Melanie clattered some silverware and pretended to be so preoccupied with the chores that she didn't hear the question. The old woman quickly forgot that she had asked a question and Allison didn't seem to notice the lack of response from Melanie.

Melanie answered Allison's questions with one syllable responses. They stayed focused on getting the job done quickly. Allison told Melanie she hoped to see her at services that evening. Melanie said she planned to be there. Allison told Melanie she was glad because the sermon was expected to be shocking. Somebody saw a copy of Rabbi Levy's sermon that was typed by his secretary.

"What's it about?" Melanie asked.

"Rumor has it that the Kings are quitting the temple," Allison explained.

"Everybody's talking about it," said Old Mrs. Benjamin.

"David King? I thought he was all involved as Chairman of the Ritual Committee," Melanie questioned.

"Oh, he is. No, it's not him. It's his brother, Marvin. Marvin doesn't agree with the rabbi about a lot of things and because their family owns the ground the temple is built on, he thinks he also owns the rabbi. You know Rabbi Levy too well. He's not for sale at any price. So there was sort of a showdown at the last Ritual Committee meeting and the rabbi told him that, if he is that unhappy, there's Temple Israel two miles east and Temple Torah one mile west and he's not a prisoner here. So the word is that they're going to quit and go elsewhere. Who could believe it?" Allison concluded prophetically.

"But his brother, David, is the chairman of that committee," Melanie stated, quizzically. "Couldn't he smooth it out?"

"Well, what I heard is that he tried but he didn't try too hard," Allison continued. "I don't think he thinks his brother is right and he also realizes his brother is an adult. So if his brother wants to quit, who is he to stop him? He doesn't seem to feel responsible for his brother's ideas or his actions. "Allison rested her case.

"Good for him," Old Mrs. Benjamin said with enthusiasm. "You have to give that David a lot of credit. He always was a sensible boy. He always uses his head. Wisdom, that's what he's got. *Wisdom.* You can't say that about too many people these days. And he's always been fair to everybody. He's a *mensch*, that's what he is, a real man in the best sense. And he's not his brother's keeper!" Mrs. Benjamin concluded with pride in the Biblical reference.

Melanie's confidence level rose. This kind of man would okay her project. This was very good news, for Melanie, anyway. It didn't sound so good for Marvin. But Melanie didn't know Marvin, so that was his problem.

As the three women put away the last remaining items in the kitchen, Melanie turned to Allison, and said," Well, I guess we're done here. I've got to hit the road. It's 11:30 already and I've got a million things I have to do today. It' s been great Allison, but do me a big favor. Lose my number."

Allison laughed good-naturedly as she gave Melanie a hug. "You were a lifesaver today, Mel. I'd have been here most of the day alone if you hadn't shown up.

There's only so much Old Mrs. Benjamin can do before she's had it!" Allison explained. "Thanks again, Mel. I'll see you tonight."

As she entered the foyer of the temple, Melanie turned quickly and headed for the sanctuary. Pushing open the huge brass doors embossed with the tablets inscribed with the Ten Commandments, Melanie rushed through, hurried across the back of the sanctuary, down the center aisle and up the five steps to the altar. When she reached the rabbi's pulpit, she searched her bag for a pen and scrap of paper. Finding them, she dashed off a note: "Dear Rabbi, Happy Shabbos! The plastics are tacky! I love you, Melanie."

Melanie folded the paper and set it up like a place card at a dining room table.

He couldn't miss it.

CHAPTER SEVENTEEN

IT WAS 11:30 am when Frank was again summoned to Dugan's office. This time he only made it as far as Dugan's secretary who sat in an outer office just outside of the door bearing the brass plate with Dugan's name engraved on it. It occurred to Frank that he had never seen a door for Ryan, Cuttler, nor Angeline.

They're probably on another floor, maybe the penthouse," Frank theorized.

"Mr. Dugan sent for me," Frank told Dugan's secretary.

"Yes, Mr. Mandell," she answered, with a military snap. "Mr. Dugan would like you to take this envelope to the same place you went last Friday and deliver it in the same manner. Your instructions are in this envelope. Mr. Dugan said to have a nice time." As she concluded, she swiveled her desk chair around and went back to work at her word processing. She was done with him.

Not bad, Frank thought as he walked down the corridor. Another half-day on Friday. Another nice little jaunt to Atlantic City. This time he would arrive with Maisy and a Louis Vuitton weekender bag, a garment bag, and a train case perched at the end of Maisy's hand. His credit was good everywhere. What a life.

After a quick call to tell Maisy to pack a few things in their new status luggage, Frank left the office. An hour later, they were on their way to Atlantic City. They stopped on the road for a quick lunch at a service area on the turnpike and arrived at the hotel at about 5:00pm.

Frank checked in and sent Maisy up to the room telling her to take a bubble bath since he'd be a while. Maisy understood that business came first and went with the bellman who, remembering escorting them to their suite last week, also took notice of the improvement of the baggage he now rolled on the luggage cart. He hoped it would also reflect an improvement in his tip. Frank overheard the bellman ask Maisy, as the elevator doors were closing, "So, did you guys hit it big last week?"

Frank walked to the sofa area, picked up a magazine and sat down with the magazine open in his lap. He looked around for Holmes, Mr. Bodyparts, but didn't see him. It was seven o'clock before Frank spotted Holmes across the lobby. They made eye contact.

Frank slipped the paperwork into the magazine and continued to thumb the magazine for another minute. Then Frank closed the magazine, tossed it carelessly on the coffee table, and stood up, glancing at his watch as if he had a date to meet. Frank walked away without turning back. Holmes took up Frank's position on the sofa, scooped up the magazine, and with it open and close to his chest, slid the papers into his breast pocket just as the elevator doors were closing with Frank inside.

Frank took the letter of instruction for him out of the envelope for the first time. It occurred to him that maybe he should have read it first but the secretary had told him to do what he did last time so it hadn't occurred to him until now that there might be something else on his instruction sheet.

The corners of Frank's mouth move imperceptibly. That was the best Frank could do for a smile. As he scanned the instruction sheet and passed the routine part he had just accomplished, he came to a paragraph that warmed his empty heart.

There's a little bonus waiting for you. Try your luck at roulette.

Frank pushed the elevator button for the casino before the doors ever opened on the floor where his room was located. The elevator stopped, the doors opened, and closed quickly as Frank pushed the buttons to speed the trip to the casino.

Once there, Frank made his way to the first roulette table he saw. They must have been watching for him on the security cameras buried in the walls and ceilings all over the casino. When Frank arrived at the table with his chips, he played red 23. It lost. He played it again. It lost again. "Why didn't they tell me what number to play?" he thought.

As Frank and the others at the roulette table were putting down their bets again, another tuxedoed man came and replaced the casino employee. "Time for my break," he said as he left. "Good luck to y'all."

Frank played '23 red' again. He lost again. And again. He decided to play it one more time before he'd try another number. This time it won. He had only ten dollars on it but it gave back a mound of chips. Frank played 27 black. It won another mound of chips. Frank randomly picked another number and dropped some chips on it. It paid off handsomely as well. He was the hero of the crowd at the table. He played one more time and learned his luck had run out.

Frank took his bucket of chips to the cashier's window. As his chips were being counted, another man came from behind the cashier, handed the cashier cash which he then counted out to Frank. "One hundred, two hundred, . . . five hundred . . . one thousand, two thousand. Have a good evening and thank you, sir. Come again."

Frank's transaction in the casino was now concluded. Not bad. Take a little drive. Have a little luck. Get down tonight. Not a bad life, at all, Frank thought.

Frank glanced at his watch. It was only 7:30. The night was young.

As he entered the towers' elevator, Frank looked back at his watch. Like the nylon zipper bags, this watch had to go. Frank would add that to his growing list of needs and desires.

CHAPTER EIGHTEEN

IT WAS NOON when Allison ran through the parking lot, jumped into her car and raced home. There was so much for her to do. She had to stop at the bakery to pick up a challah for their own Shabbat dinner at home. She had to pick up Josh from his playgroup and Jennifer from her sister-in-law, Dawn. Somewhere in between there were the quick stops at the library to return books and a quick drive through Dairy Barn's drive-up window to buy milk, eggs, ice cream, and a bouquet of fresh flowers that they sold from a wire display rack between the cookies and the breads. She'd do all of that before she picked up the kids.

By the time she made all of her stops, and got the kids home, it was mid-afternoon. Josh and Jennie could be counted on to take naps for the next couple of hours and that would give Allison time to get herself and the house ready for Shabbat.

Their eighteen year old au pair, Sylvie, was a great help. She was the oldest daughter in a large French family and was descended from the aristocracy. Her father was a surgeon and her mother a judge. No one could believe she was spending her time as the scullery maid to an American family where her duties included housecleaning and diaper-changing.

Allison had given Sylvie the day off since she would expect her to be available throughout the entire weekend, night and day beginning at sundown Friday evening, to watch the children and keep the house in order while Allison and Dave attended services, entertained friends and family and generally socialized.

While the children napped in the quiet house, Allison set the table for Shabbat dinner, a task she enjoyed and saved for herself, put the finishing touches on the dinner she had prepared the night before and readied for the oven, and went to her room to lay out her clothes for the evening. Having accomplished all of this, Allison got ready to take a shower so she'd be out before the children awoke from their naps. Her terrycloth robe was placed on the hook on the bathroom door and her Shalimar shower lotion was placed on the marble ledge in the shower stall.

Sylvie arrived home having made her rounds of the beauty salon for a styling and the library for a new batch of children's books to practice her English. Since she had the day off, she thought she'd take advantage of the opportunity to enjoy the deck and the comfortable lounge chairs in the beautiful garden of the Shapiro house.

As if on cue, the telephone rang just as Allison was about to step into the shower. Allison grabbed her robe and, sliding it on, exited the steamy bathroom to answer the phone.

Sylvie, hearing the water running in the shower upstairs, ran to the phone as well. As she lifted the receiver, she heard Allison say, "Hello." Allison struggled to get the receiver past her shower cap, not realizing that the reason for the hollowness she heard through the receiver was the result of Sylvie being on the extension.

"Hello, sweetheart. Whatcha doin?" the deep, raspy voice asked.

"I'm about to get into the shower."

"I guess that makes this an obscene phone call," he chuckled in a forced laugh.

"David, stop it. I think you are wonderful but you have to leave me alone. I'm married. I've got two little kids. If I had met you first maybe things could have been different. But this is not going to work," Allison rambled on.

"Tell me you love him and I'll never bother you again. Tell me the truth. Say it," he dared her.

Allison fell silent. The truth was that there was a David in her life that she loved. But it was not David Shapiro. It was David King.

"The water's running," is all that Allison could bring herself to say.

"I love you, Allison. I'm sorry my timing stinks in your life. But do we have to throw away what we feel for each other because I had the misfortune of showing up late in *your* life. It's not too late, my love. We don't have to spend the rest of our lives apart to pay for what's happened in the last five years." His lecture stopped abruptly.

"Oh, God, David. I can't handle this."

"Allison, meet me Monday. I'll be in Manhattan for a breakfast meeting at seven A.M. I'll be done by ten, ten-thirty the latest. Meet me in the lobby lounge at the Algonquin Hotel on 44th Street between 5th and 6th at eleven. It'll be too early for a drink in their Blue Bar although it'll be 5 o'clock somewhere! We'll have coffee! Promise me you'll be there."

"I'll be there," is all that Allison said. But it was enough. Allison hung up.

David King hung up. Sylvie hung up. Allison sat on the edge of the bed staring at the phone. Dear God, she thought. What have I done?

CHAPTER NINETEEN

Melanie arrived at the temple at 7:30 pm, thirty minutes early for Sabbath Services. The sanctuary was almost empty. Melanie surveyed the rows of pews determining where she wanted to sit. She finally settled on the seventh row center aisle seat on the left side. Because of the incline of the floor, her seat almost gave her eye contact with the rabbi when he was standing at his pulpit.

Melanie settled in and watched the arriving worshippers fill their seats. A murmur of voices greeting one another with good wishes for the Sabbath filled the air.

Melanie noticed the arrival of past presidents of the congregation and their husbands and wives filing in. The president of the Sisterhood arrived and was immediately surrounded by adoring fans. Melanie could not relate to any of that part of temple life. It was the spiritual side that motivated her to be here. Nothing more.

As she watched the parade of the politically-involved march past, Melanie observed a certain rhythm to their movement down the aisles. The past presidents marched with a certain strut and the current presidents of the Congregation's Sisterhood and Brotherhood, moved with a swagger. Melanie wondered if this was obvious only to her.

As she sat waiting and watching, Melanie wondered how her cousin, Maisy was doing. It wasn't that long ago that Maisy was married right here. And those same tacky plastic flowers were still on the bema. The more things change, the more they stay the same.

The rabbi appeared. Melanie looked at her watch. It was five minutes before eight. She watched him to see if he saw her note. He disappointed her. He didn't even stop at his pulpit. Instead, he walked down the five steps from the bema and walked up the center aisle of the sanctuary, shaking hands, kissing cheeks, wishing people Gutte Shabbos. He stopped to wish every joy to the family of the Bar Mitzvah boy and to express his deepest sympathy to a family who was in a period of mourning, stopping at each member of the group to express his sadness for the loss of a husband, a father, an uncle, and a son. The generations were there, on both sides of the aisle, to share the joy, on one side, and, on the other side, to bear up under the sadness that is delivered into every life. The presence of the congregants and the rabbi heightened the joy and focused the mourning on the continuum of the life cycle, easing the pain only in that it was no longer focused on "Why is this happening to me?" and elevating it to one more plateau in the lifecycle.

As David King entered through the brass doors, Melanie thought how marvelous he was. What a wonderful family he came from, she thought, to have given this community this temple in which to celebrate and memorialize their comings and goings, their achievements and their sacred moments. He was a man above the crowd. She had to know him better.

The mother of the Bar Mitzvah boy was called to light and bless the Sabbath Candles. The rabbi began the service. At the appropriate moment, David King presented the young man with a Kiddush cup, the ceremonial cup for blessings. As David returned to his seat, the congregants sat frozen. Not a cough, sneeze or clearing of a throat could be heard. The first shoe was about to fall and everyone there knew it.

"I wish to tell you a story as we welcome the Sabbath," the rabbi began. "It's a short story but it is appropriate tonight as we reflect on what has happened to us and with us in the last week and as we prepare to go forward to meet the challenges of the coming week.

"There are always those among us who are so filled with self-importance that they believe that their presence, or lack of it, will significantly change the world or even stop it from spinning. So it is with a case we face this week.

"Our temple has been blessed with caring and generous families who have done much to be supportive of our congregation. We all hold these families and their individual members in the highest regard. However, this week we have been faced with a difference of opinion between one member and myself. And my opinion on this particular issue is not negotiable and not for sale. I am the spiritual leader of this congregation. I report to a higher authority than the temple board. And, for that reason, I cannot agree to do things because they are popular. I cannot agree to do things because they are cost-effective. I cannot agree to do things because powerful people in the temple or the community think I should. I can only agree to do things because they are the correct things to do.

In this case, the correct thing to do is to do just the opposite of that which I am being asked to do. And therein lays the controversy.

"For me, it is so very simple and there is no controversy. Unfortunately, there are those who see a more expedient path which I cannot take. My answer, then, is: walk with me on the path I believe to be correct or find another path to walk by yourself because I am just not going there with you!"

The congregants sat motionless. It seemed like everyone had forgotten to breathe. The rabbi stopped speaking and the huge high-ceilinged room was as silent as it was when Melanie was there alone earlier in the day.

"As a result of my stand, one of our esteemed members has indicated that he is no longer interested in being a temple member. Many of you will be surprised by my reaction: There are other temples. Go join one of them.

"I will not be intimidated or bullied. I will not be coerced. And if you think that the temple and temple life as we know it will come to a crashing halt because of this person's absence, let me assure you that nothing of the kind will happen.

"I am aware that this person believes himself to be indispensable. I am convinced that many of you may also hold that belief.

"So now let me recite to you a lesson from the rabbis of the ages about indispensability. There once was a very small village in Eastern Europe in the middle ages. And in this village, there was a very wealthy man. Because of his wealth, he was able to give generously to the poor and to the synagogue and for these reasons he enjoyed considerable power. His opinions were respected as truth and wisdom. Often, his opinions were neither.

"One day, the wealthy man found himself in the middle of a great controversy. He wanted the new town well built near his home for his convenience. The doctor wanted the well built near his home where he treated patients to be convenient in emergencies.

"The two men, both important to the community, brought their controversy to the village rabbi. The rabbi listened to both sides. It was clear to the rabbi that there was no contest here. Clearly, the well should be placed near the doctor's home.

"The wealthy man was furious and threatened to move to another village. The rabbi answered that there were many lovely villages to choose from and all within twenty kilometers.

"'How can you suggest such a thing?' the wealthy man exploded. 'I am indispensable to this village.'

"The rabbi leaned forward, looked the wealthy man directly in his eyes and said, 'There is an ancient test handed down to us through the generations. This test will show you just how indispensable you are.' The wealthy man listened attentively. The rabbi continued, handing him a wooden bucket. 'Take this bucket and go to the town well with it. Fill the bucket to the top with water. Then put the bucket on the ground and kneel down next to it. Roll your sleeve all the way up your arm. Then make a fist and plunge your hand into the bucket until your knuckles touch to the bottom. Hold your hand there for five minutes. Then, pull your arm out of the bucket. Carefully examine the contents of the bucket for the hole you leave behind which represents how indispensable you are.'"

The rabbi had concluded his story and his sermon. He stood there, silently, for only a moment and then said, "All rise." The service concluded with a joyful song welcoming the Sabbath.

CHAPTER TWENTY

THE ROWS OF worshippers emptied in an orderly fashion starting from the front row. The Rabbi came down from the bema and, shaking hands with the members of the Bar Mitzvah family, led them out into the aisle and sent them on their way to the Oneg Shabbat waiting for them in the adjoining area. Each row of congregants and guests followed.

The rabbi blessed the wine and the challah and, for the next hour, everyone socialized over wine, cake, cookies, fruit, coffee and soda.

Melanie now began to feel good about the time she had given to help prepare for this lovely tradition. She started to feel guilty about giving Allison a hard time about asking for her help.

Melanie's guilt could not begin to compare to what Allison was feeling. Allison had slipped out of the sanctuary, while the congregation was singing, to help unwrap the platters of cake and cookies from their cellophane enclosures. As she emerged from the kitchen where she stored the wrappings for later use, she was met by her husband, Dave, who was waiting for her. Together, they circulated around the room, coffee cups in hand, chatting with Dave's sister, Dawn, and her husband, Fred. The foursome widened their circle to include other couples and singles who stopped to chat with them. The conversation would start again and again with each new entrant and would go from a quick analysis of the rabbi's sermon, a reaction to the news of Marv King leaving the temple, to who was driving carpool this week and what was happening in community and world events.

Allison tried to stay absorbed in the chitchat. In other circles around the room, she and Dave were the topic of conversation. They were a stunning couple and people enjoyed commenting on how beautiful she looked, how handsome he was, and what a great job she had done as Chairwoman of the Oneg Committee.

When David King entered the room, there was an audible hush. Everything seemed to stop. Could he really not care if his brother left the temple? Was he glad his brother wouldn't be there anymore, leaving him all the more important? Was it better to say, "Gee, David, sorry to hear about this business with your brother," or was it better to say nothing? Was David embarrassed by it or did he divorce himself from his brother's actions? No one really knew what the right thing to say was. So, most people just said something neutral like, "Gutte Shabbos, David, how are ya doin'?" and moved on from there.

David stopped at the little circle that included Allison, Dave, Dawn and Fred. Allison's heart dropped into her shoes. Her face flushed. Her throat tightened and her palms began to sweat.

"Quite a sermon," David King commented, disarming everyone.

"Sure was," Fred answered.

They were all saved by another couple standing there who asked Dawn a question about the elementary school soccer team and the subject changed at once.

David tried to make eye contact with Allison. Allison kept her gaze firmly riveted on her coffee cup. Then she excused herself and went into the kitchen for safety.

David followed her.

"Can I help you with anything?" he asked.

"You can get out of here," she answered.

"I'll see you Monday," he whispered.

Without looking at him, Allison nodded. How could she have this conversation with him in the temple of all places, she thought. How did she get herself into this mess?

Melanie went into the temple kitchen to look for Allison to say goodnight and silently practiced saying, "Lose my number the next time you need help setting up!" Instead, she put her kidding-on-the-level sense of humor away lest it be misunderstood and, finding Allison there, wished her a Shabbat Shalom. As Melanie started to make her exit, Allison seized the opportunity to ask for another charitable favor.

"Mel, the Temple nursery school is planning a little outing on Monday and they're short a chaperone. I can't be there so I said I'd ask around and see if I could find someone for them. It'll only be for an hour. They're going over to that horse farm in Nissequogue where that horse that jumped six foot fences lived. You might enjoy it. Somebody wrote a book about that horse that was read to the kids and they're going to see his descendents that now live on the farm. The jumper's name was Flying Dutchman. The kids love the story and you'll really enjoy the trip," Allison implored.

"Sorry, Al. I have my yearly physical scheduled for Monday. They check me into the hospital and I'm there for most of the day. In fact, I just bumped into my doctor at the Oneg who said, quite ominously, that he's looking forward to seeing me on Monday. I don't want to read too much into that but I really hate seeing my physicians at social events!" Melanie chuckled.

"Gee, that's too bad for the kids and for you," Allison replied. "I'll keep asking! I'm sure I'll find somebody!"

"Believe me, given the choice, there's no contest! This is one appointment I would prefer to swap for a trip to the horse farm."

They said their goodnights and Allison internalized one more level of guilt for planning not to be there for the nursery school trip.

CHAPTER TWENTY-ONE

THE ROUTINES BROUGHT by Monday pushed the weekend into a distant memory.

Allison left the house as soon as the nursery school bus had whisked Josh from the driveway. Sylvie was at home with Jennifer and would be there with lunch waiting when Josh returned at noon. Allison felt emotionally pulled and tugged as she got into her SAAB and drove to the Long Island Railroad station. She knew the right thing to do but she didn't have the strength or discipline to do it. David King was a man like none she had ever known before. How could she cheat herself out of the excitement, the attention, the affection he brought to her life? She was compelled to go and meet him in Manhattan.

Allison parked her SAAB at the Long Island Railroad station, grabbed her purse and the sections of Sunday's Newsday she hadn't finished reading, and headed for the train platform. She turned the pages hoping to find an advice column that would tell her what she already knew, advice that would turn her around, literally, and send her home before her life changed forever.

As she waited on the platform, Allison lied to herself and knew she was lying. She rehearsed how she would meet David with a handshake and, over coffee, secluded in a corner of the lobby lounge hidden by a plant and column, rationally explain why they would never spend time alone together again. She would talk about her husband, her children, her home, her commitment to all of that and why there could be no space for David in that picture. She would tell him how wonderful it had been knowing him and how much she enjoyed knowing him but that their relationship could go nowhere and must stop before it begins. And all the while she planned her monologue, she realized how impossible it would be for her to say any of those things to David King, the love of her life.

Allison was so absorbed in her thoughts that she didn't even remember stepping onto the train and settling into a window seat.

All the way to the city, she replayed in her mind how she and David had met working on a temple committee. She remembered how fairly he treated every committee member, listening to each one with patience and respect regardless of how ridiculous some of their ideas and comments seemed to Allison. She was touched by his warmth and charm and moved by his straightforward and honest approach to bringing consensus to the group at each meeting, helping them to make good decisions for the good of the congregation.

She couldn't put her finger on the moment when she knew she loved him. It might have been at the first meeting she attended. There was so much tension and anger around that table with each member trying to wield power and influence the inevitable vote about which Allison remembered nothing. What she did remember was David's remark to the committee: "It seems to me that, although there are twelve of us here, I have counted thirteen opinions!" The group burst into laughter and the tension was broken. The mood and attitudes shifted to one of cooperation to forge a plan everyone could accept. David's command of the situation reflected the things Allison found most attractive in a man: intelligence, wisdom and humor. At that moment, as David seized control of the group, he also seized control of her heart. Allison knew, in that moment, that her life would never be the same.

As the towns of Long Island flashed by the train window, Allison relived triumphs, struggles, meetings, projects in development, achievements and awards that resulted from her collaborations with David and the committees they served on.

Somewhere in the midst of their attention to a higher purpose, they bonded. Fighting the good fight was an uphill climb but doing it together bonded them. Their weekly Ritual Committee meeting ended at the Village Diner and, over coffee and bagels, they would review the meeting like theatre critics. Even their painful setbacks caused by stupid obstacles presented by brain-dead committee members was cause for laughter as David put it all into perspective, sorted out what had happened from what needed to be done next and applied his practical philosophy of life to every situation.

Their weekly meetings at first ended with handshakes, later with kisses on cheeks, and then graduated to goodbye hugs. At no time did David forget that he was meeting with Mrs. Dave Shapiro. At no time did Allison encourage David King to enter her heart. It was just something that happened somewhere in the battle when the sides were drawn and they embraced one another in the good fight. Their "sum-up sessions," as David called them, had become the high point of Allison's week.

Allison never expected her feelings for David to be returned. Everyone said that David no longer had a heart. As a shrewd businessman, he was described as having no conscience. As a person, he was known as cold and emotionless. But who could blame him. David's life was like the story of Job. He was a person with everything one could wish or pray for. He was intelligent, handsome, charming, witty, sometimes even zany, cavorting about in slapstick comedian style, completely out of his carefully created image. He had impeccable taste in everything from clothing, furniture, food, wine and every detail in his life plus he could afford the best and used his wealth to create a perfect world around him.

But David could only control the things that money could buy. Outside of the perfect dollhouse he had created for himself to live in and control, David's life was cold and empty. He had loved once, long ago, and planned to marry his high school sweetheart. They met in fourth grade, dated in junior high school, and got serious in high school. She was the perfect complement to David's plans for his future. She was head cheerleader and star of the senior show. She had the voice of an angel and the poise of a seasoned Broadway actress. She was named Whitney, after her world famous architect grandfather, and inherited an abundance of artistic talent which she chose to exhibit through the performing arts.

She played Maria in the senior show production of "West Side Story." The entire community turned out to see it. Even among this sophisticated audience of Broadway theatre-goers, no one could believe the incredible acting skills and nightingale voice of the lead actress, this high school student. She was so skilled and talented and belied her eighteen years. David was so proud that she was his girl and looked forward to their plans to marry after they both graduated from college.

Graduation ceremonies took place two weeks after the rave reviews of the senior show were published. The few people who hadn't attended one of the six performances knew they had missed something special and regretted their laziness about getting tickets. As Whitney walked up on the stage to accept her diploma, she was met with a standing ovation and cheers from all assembled there as a special thank you and vote of encouragement from a community that knew it would one day be made proud by her, this native daughter.

But no one there was more proud of Whitney than David King. Whitney was the missing part of his personal puzzle. She was the piece that would make everything complete.

Three other couples joined David and Whitney for the traditional after-prom festivities. They left the prom early, went into New York City, hit a couple of clubs, took a ride on the Staten Island Ferry to watch the sunrise and then headed home in the limousine that had been rented for their pleasure and safety.

The limo dropped each of them at home. They would all change into swimsuits and head for Jones Beach with blankets and suntan lotion to spend the day there.

They were all going to meet at David's house where they would decide who would go in which car. David's family had a huge driveway with lots of room for the cars that got left behind. Whitney and three others were being picked up in the graduation gift of one of the guys, a metallic blue convertible, and shuttled to David's house.

David stood in the shade of a huge weeping willow tree on his front lawn waiting for the two cars that would gather everyone together to begin their trip to the beach. It was only ten o'clock in the morning and it was already blazing hot. With orange juice in hand, David leaned against the tree, checking his watch impatiently. Two kids arrived. They waited together for the other car, not wanting to call anyone's house at this early hour. Girls take forever to get changed, David thought.

Mrs. King appeared on the front porch and walked down the path. David remembered thinking it was odd for his mother to come out to the driveway in her robe and slippers. She was a very proper lady and disapproved of immodest behavior. The look on her face told David that something was wrong. Mrs. King was up early making sure David was okay but staying on the sidelines so that he didn't feel her mothering presence. She had the radio on and just learned that there had been an accident. The driver and the front seat passenger were killed and the three backseat passengers were in critical condition in the hospital. The driver tried to race a train across the tracks at an unguarded crossing. His timing was bad and there was a collision. David knew who was driving. But who was in the front seat? Mrs. King said that they had not released names because the families were not all notified yet.

Before Mrs. King could finish speaking, David had jumped into his car and raced out of the driveway to the hospital, praying that

Whitney was a backseat passenger. When he arrived at the hospital, David learned that his worst nightmare was a reality. Whitney had died in the crash.

David was numb with denial. But as the numbness wore off, David vowed never to care again, never to love again, never to expose himself to the kind of pain he felt losing Whitney. And the only way to assure himself that this could never happen to him again was to protect himself from ever loving anyone again. David had been successful at putting his emotions in a steel vault until he met Allison, the wife of Dave Shapiro and the mother of Jennifer and Joshua. His feelings for Allison made no sense to David King and contradicted every conviction he held. It was something that happened in spite of his principles and commitment to staying emotionally aloof.

Nothing in the newspaper touched Allison. Leaving the newspaper on the seat of the train, Allison got off at Penn Station and hailed a taxi to the Algonquin. She had to find a way to keep her marriage and her family in tact without hurting David. She couldn't be the one to injure him when he was finally coming out of his self-imposed prison. There had to be a way to do this right so no one got hurt. She couldn't hurt Dave and the kids but she couldn't hurt David either. There were too many victims here. Not to mention her own agony.

CHAPTER TWENTY-TWO

AS SOON AS Allison's Saab had turned the corner, Sylvie left her spot at the living room window and raced to the telephone in the kitchen. Systematically, she called her two best au pair friends who inhabited homes in the community. Starting with her French friend first, and then working her way to the English young woman, living and working in nearby homes, Sylvie shared the exciting bit of gossip she had learned today: Allison Shapiro and David King are lovers and they are meeting, as we speak, at the Algonquin in New York City.

The rumor spread like a fire in Malibu. Au pairs told their host mothers who called their friends who called their friends. The two au pairs that Sylvie called each called several friends of theirs. Within the hour more than one hundred people in the community "knew" that Allison and David were having an affair. To date, all that had transpired between them were platonic hugs and kisses on the cheek and the words "I love you" spoken only by David.

There was little place for truth in the rumor mill. No one really cared about truth anyway. A good story like this one would keep the community entertained for months. There had to be something going on there. After all, Sylvie lived in the house. Who would know better?

Sylvie finished her last call just as Jennifer woke up. She went up to the nursery and lovingly lifted the baby from her crib. The pink wallpaper reflected Jennifer's rosy complexion. The baby cooed as Sylvie placed soft kisses on her stomach, holding Jennifer in the air above Sylvie's head. Slowly lowering her, Sylvie kissed the baby's face making little circles of kisses. Jennifer giggled, encouraging Sylvie to continue.

"Ooh, *ma petite choux. Tu es mon enfant.* Come, *ma cherie, Maman* will prepare something for you to eat."

How nice it would be to be the mother of these two children, the lady of this beautiful house, the wife of handsome Dave Shapiro, Sylvie thought. It wouldn't take much for her to charm Dave. Especially now.

CHAPTER TWENTY-THREE

Davids meeting ended earlier than he expected. He got everything he wanted. He left the building and headed uptown. The extra time gave him the opportunity to do a little shopping along the way. He picked up a shirt and tie at Versace before continuing on to the Algonquin.

David was enjoying his coffee in the comfortable elegance of the hotel's lobby lounge when he saw Allison approaching. It was the perfect atmosphere to spend time with her. David knew she'd feel like they were in the great hall of a castle in Ireland with their butler taking care of their needs. He rose to greet her and, glancing at his watch said, "Right on time!"

"You'd say that if I were two hours late," Allison quipped.

David beamed as he looked at her. He was truly happy in her presence. He leaned forward to kiss her on the cheek but Allison stepped back.

"Let's me a order coffee for you," he said.

While David had a view of the entry to the hotel's lobby, Allison's seat made David the focus. Once cocooned in their space, for David and Allison, in that moment, there were no other people on the planet. The waiter cleared his throat, trying to penetrate the invisible shield that clearly cut them off from everything around them.

David ordered coffee for them and an assortment of cheeses, crackers and fresh fruit. The waiter left. The silence between them began.

Allison was afraid to say anything. David was afraid to push too quickly lest he lose her. Neither said a word. The silence was awkward.

The waiter brought the coffee in a stylish silver pot and the assorted cheeses and fruit on a triangular white dish. Allison felt removed and disconnected from her life and David seemed to her like the prince of childhood fairytales who was suppose to rescue the damsel in distress. Allison loved the pampering and the attention. And she was so afraid of the love she felt for David that she was sure would ruin her life and, maybe, his.

"Coffee's good," David said, breaking the silence.

"Yes," Allison responded, thinking, Dear God, get me out of here. Why did I ever come here?

"Look, Allison, I don't even know where to start. I thought my life was over more than twenty years ago. I never thought I could or would allow myself to care about anybody. And then I met you. I can't explain what happened. I wouldn't have planned this for anything in the world. I didn't even want this to happen to me. I don't need complications in my life. I've learned to live in a little world I've created for myself. It's a perfect world for me and I have everything I want. At least I had everything I wanted for a long time. And then I met you. And you present a major complication.

"It's not my style to walk away from something I want, "David continued. "I know you care about me. I see it in every move you make when I'm there. You are a wonderful woman and I want you in my life. Tell me what I have to do to get you to leave Dave. I'll do whatever it takes. There's been chemistry between us from the first moment. We're cut from the same piece of cloth. Dave's a nice guy but you don't love him. I can see it and I can see that you care about me in a way that you have never cared about him."

"David, please stop," Allison interrupted. "You don't know me. You only think you know me. You're right. I do feel something special for you."

"It's more than something special," he cut in.

"Let me finish, David," she continued. "It's true that Dave and I have drifted apart. I think that has something to do with me being so busy with the house and the kids and the temple and he's so busy with his business. But that's no reason for me to leave him. I took vows and I believe in those vows."

"Allison, tell me you love him. Tell me you don't love me. Do that and I will never bother you again."

"I can't tell you either of those things."

"I don't get it," David said, shaking his head in dismay.

"What don't you get? I love you with all my heart. But I have to do what's right. I can't do this to Dave. It's wrong"

"No, I don't believe that. Nothing that feels this good could be wrong," David replied. "Allison," David continued, taking her hand in his across the table, "I will love, honor, protect, and provide for you and your children, and, if we're lucky, for our children as well, forever and ever in this life and the next. I will pamper and spoil you and I will cherish every moment we have together now and always. And those are my vows to you. I have known love and I have lost it. I will not lose it again. God put you in my life for a reason. We have so much to give each other."

Tears rolled down Allison's face. She was glad that she faced only David and the corner of the room.

"I'm so confused. I love you, David, but I can't do this."

"Are you happy with him?'

Allison remained silent.

"Are you there because of a sense of obligation? You're not obligated to an unhappy but dutiful life! This is not the middle ages. You have options. I'll get you a wonderful apartment with three bedrooms, a great view, and all the playgrounds, swimming pools, shops, and parking you need to have every convenience in the world for you and the children. I'll take a one year lease and pay the whole thing in advance so you won't have to worry about what happens next. That'll give you plenty of time to get a divorce and time for us time to find the perfect house for the four of us. As soon as your divorce is final, we'll get married, take a fabulous honeymoon and move into the house together. And I promise you, you will never regret it. I will devote myself to making you happy. You are my second chance, Allison. I will see to it that you have all the best life has to offer."

Allison was weeping uncontrollably. She loved her children. She loved David. And it was true that she felt nothing for Dave. Dave was the perfect husband of choice by her mother. He was everything her mother thought a husband should be. First and foremost, he was very handsome. He was tall, slim, had a college degree, they were the same religion and he professed his love for Allison. What else could a mother want for her daughter? Unfortunately, no one ever asked Allison if she cared about Dave enough to want to spend the rest of her life with him. She accepted his two carat engagement ring along with his good looks and his promising future, telling herself that she could make a happy life with these ingredients and trust herself to stay faithful and loyal to him. She could hear her mother's words saying, "It's better when the man loves the woman more because you know you can trust yourself and, if he loves you more, you'll be able to trust him too."

So much for Mother's Ideology.

"I don't know what to do, David. You're making me crazy," Allison sobbed. "I have to get out of here."

David grabbed her arm as she stood up. "Please think about my offer. Please think about us. I'll call you tomorrow. I love you, Allison."

Allison tried to compose herself. She turned and walked through the lobby of the Algonquin into the breeze blowing across town. She signaled the doorman for a taxi and retraced her steps on the LIRR to her home on Long Island. By the time she pulled into her driveway, her makeup had been freshened and the signs of her upsetting day were gone.

She had plenty of time to get ready for dinner and Dave's arrival home. She needed all of that time to put the events of the day aside and move forward as if they never happened.

CHAPTER TWENTY-FOUR

TUESDAY MORNING COULDN'T come fast enough for Melanie. She dressed methodically, choosing a business suit, tailored shirt, and cufflinks, with meticulous attention to the coordination of every detail and the remaining accessories necessary to create the image of, "I mean business and I plan to get my way."

Without thinking, she chose the same outfit she wore to the last meeting she attended where she needed to persuade twelve people to vote her way and was successful. Somewhere inside she knew this was a powerful outfit that would work its magic again.

The receptionist at David King's office told her that David was running on schedule and would be available for their eleven o'clock appointment precisely at eleven. Melanie was not surprised that this meticulous man ran his business life with the same exactness he displayed in his wardrobe. She felt reassured by her own attention to detail in her outfit and her early arrival for their appointment.

As the ship's clock in the reception area began to strike eleven tiny bell sounds, the receptionist told Melanie that David King would see her now and led her down a long hallway to the corner office. David stood from behind his mammoth desk and walked around it to greet Melanie. The entire wall behind his desk was glass from floor to twelve-foot ceiling bathing his office in the bright glare of morning sunlight. It wasn't until David was in the center of the room that he came into focus for Melanie. With a hearty handshake, David greeted Melanie and escorted her over to the large-pillowed sofa on the other side of the huge office. As David settled into a leather wing-backed chair, Melanie glanced quickly around the office, taking in the cherry mahogany conference table and colonial credenza, the floor sculptures and framed artwork that lined the walls, and the plaques and awards that were mounted on shelves in the sofa area where they were seated.

"Your office is beautiful," Melanie began. "And I truly appreciated your taking time from your busy day to meet with me."

"It comes with the territory," David said, smiling warmly at Melanie. It was the kind of smile that made her feel like she had known David forever and that she could tell him anything without fear of embarrassment. "I knew when I undertook the responsibility of Ritual Chairman that it was more than an honorary title. So what brings you here today, Melanie?"

David leaned back in his comfortable chair and crossed his arms across his chest while he paid close attention to Melanie's explanation of what she wanted to do and how she would accomplish it. David surprised her, when she completed her story, by saying, "What do you do when you're not on your flowers crusade, Melanie?"

"What do you mean?" Melanie asked, affronted by David's lack of focus on the subject at hand.

"Well, you just made a very persuasive argument and an enthusiastic presentation about something completely inconsequential in the scheme of things. Nonetheless, you motivated me and, apparently the rabbi, or you wouldn't be here now. You also showed a serious degree of perseverance or you wouldn't have gotten to see me at all. So my question is, what do you do with all of those skills when you're not worrying about flowers?"

"I'm not sure whether to be flattered by your interest or insulted by your ignoring why I came to see you," Melanie shot back.

"I have no reason to want to flatter you, Melanie. I'm just making an observation. I am truly impressed with every move you have made since you walked through that door. But you don't have to tell me if you don't want to," David concluded.

David's reverse psychology pushed the right buttons in Melanie. Suddenly, there seemed no reason why she shouldn't tell David where she acquired her skills.

"Well, what exactly do you want to know?" she asked. And before he could respond, she found herself telling him that her powers of persuasion began to develop at the age of four when she would convince her grandfather, at their weekly Friday afternoon visits, that they should visit the jewelry shop up the street to do a little shopping for bracelets, necklaces and the like.

David smiled warmly as he listened to Melanie talk about those early memories, identifying with his own memories of a stern grandfather who always gave in to David's demands for two ice creams from the Good Humor truck when all the other grandchildren were allowed only one. The sweetness of their memories were reflected in both Melanie's and David's faces.

"Tell me about your education and your business experience," David inquired.

"What is this, a job interview?" Melanie asked.

"You never know," was David's reply.

Intrigued by David's motivation, Melanie continued. What could be nicer than someone being interested in you, she thought. Melanie babbled on about her education and her life experiences uninterruptedly for about twenty minutes, finally getting to the immediate present.

"So, when my father died, I left my sales and marketing position and took over my father's business which I inherited as the only heir. It was a struggle just to pick up the reigns of that wild stallion but, after about six months, I got the hang of it and knew enough to know this was not what I wanted to do with my life. So I sold everything: the business, the real estate, the interests in other businesses, everything. It took over a year to clean house and become liquid. That's when I took some of the money and set up a foundation in my father's memory to do good things for people who need help. Everything we give goes to deserving individuals, not to institutions. I meet regularly with the board of trustees I established to review how the money is invested, how much we have to distribute, and where the money is going. For a while it took all of my time but now it all runs quite efficiently so I have time to bother about things like flowers in the sanctuary," Melanie concluded.

David King leaned back in his chair, arms folded across his chest. His expression exuded warmth and charm. He beamed a broad but relaxed smile, the smile of a satisfied man. Melanie could not help being drawn into the emotional stage he had set with her as the starring player. Her eyes were fixed on him, waiting to see where this was going.

"Melanie," he began," I'm impressed. And I have to tell you that I don't impress easy."

Melanie believed him. His remarks lifted her spirit. Only her father had said things to her that made her feel this way. What a secure man he had to be, to be able to make that statement, Melanie thought.

"Melanie, I know you came here to talk about flowers for the bema so let's get that out of the way first. Although I am the committee chairman, the person you need to speak with about anything related to decor is Miriam Posner. My secretary can give you her telephone number. Call her to discuss your idea.

"Next, you are correct. What started out as your flowers agenda became my agenda. My company is growing and expanding like wildfire. I need people like you who have sales and marketing skills, a brain to go with it and the motivation to stay focused and move projects along. I feel like the engineer of a long freight train and I'm pulling a heavy load alone."

David King had used all of the right words to touch Melanie's imagination and her heart. How could she not help him?

Melanie visualized being the powerful caboose pushing from behind like the illustrations in the picture books of her childhood.

"I'd like you to work with me, Melanie. I can pay you well, but it doesn't sound like money is an issue here. In any event, I'll pay you fairly and give you opportunities and challenges to keep your life exciting. You stick with me and I'll make you a star."

"David, I don't even know what your company does!"

"Tell you what. I have a noon appointment and the rest of the day I'm tied up.

How about getting together tomorrow?"

"Sorry, I have to be in the city tomorrow for a trustees meeting," Melanie replied, embarrassed to say she was making the trip to get a haircut and do some shopping.

"Can you meet me for breakfast Friday morning? How about seven-thirty at the Village Diner? I have a nine o'clock meeting but that should give us enough time for me to give you some insights into where I'm at, where I want to go and how you can help me get there," David suggested.

"It doesn't cost me anything to listen," Melanie replied, subtly stating her lack of commitment to anything. "I'll be there. Seven-thirty, Friday, at the diner," she repeated.

Melanie thanked David for his time and his interest in her and left his office, stopping at the receptionist's desk for Miriam Posner's telephone number. What an incredible day this had turned out to be. Melanie was starting to get a little bored with her life. She had to be to become so consumed over flowers for the sanctuary, she thought. Maybe she had lost sight of her own life since her father's death. Maybe the temple flowers were the path she was supposed to take to lead her to David King and a whole new direction for her life. Life was a mysterious series of bends in the road, she thought. This could be a whole new adventure.

As soon as Melanie arrived home, she called Miriam Posner.

"Posner residence," the young voice replied with a French accent.

"This is Melanie Cohen. Is Miriam Posner in, please?"

"One moment, please."

A nasal," Hello," interrupted the silence.

"Is this Miriam?"

"Yes, who is this?"

"This is Melanie Cohen. I'm a member of Temple . . . ." She was interrupted by Miriam's reply.

"Yes, Melanie, I know who you are. I knew your father. We served on several temple and community boards together. How can I help you, dear?"

""Well, I have an idea I'd like to talk with you about. Do you think you could make some time for me this week to discuss it?"

"What is it about, dear?"

Miriam's warmth and friendliness relaxed Melanie. She felt she had the attention of an ally. This was going to be easy. Melanie simply replied that she had an idea for the sanctuary that the rabbi liked. She retraced the steps of having been sent by the rabbi to David King and then by David to Miriam and here she was.

"How is tomorrow for you, dear?" Miriam asked.

"No, sorry, I have an appointment in the city tomorrow. How is Thursday for you?" Melanie asked. "About ten-thirty?"

"Thursday it is, then," Miriam answered with enthusiasm. "I'm looking forward to seeing you, my dear. Do you know how to get to my house?"

Melanie wrote down all of the twists, turns and landmarks that Miriam described as quickly and legibly as she could and, saying goodbye to Miriam, placed the directions in her wallet so they could not be misplaced. *What a productive day*, Melanie thought. *It's wonderful to be alive.*

CHAPTER TWENTY-FIVE

THE CORRIDORS OF RCA & D bustled with activity when Frank arrived at work. The normal subdued atmosphere was replaced with the murmuring conversations and administrative staff rustling papers in the hallways, rushing memos from office to office. Frank couldn't imagine what could have caused the commotion. The expressions on faces were as grim as the day outside.

As he approached his office, his secretary stopped him at the doorway. "Mr. Dugan wants to see you now, Frank," she commanded. As Frank started to step through the doorway to hang up his dripping raincoat, she continued with, "Don't waste any time, Frank. They're waiting for you."

Terror struck in Frank's heart. Should he run now ? What could he have done? The image of the black room flashed into Frank's mind. His brow showed the level of his fear. He took a handkerchief from his pocket and wiped the sweat that had just appeared there, saying, "I can't believe how hard it's raining outside," knowing that his umbrella had kept his face dry.

Frank walked quickly down the corridor while his secretary buzzed ahead to let them know he was on the way. It was clear that this was not a good day to keep Mr. Dugan waiting.

"Frank, my boy! Glad you're here. Have a seat, "Mr. Dugan directed.

"Glad to be of service, sir," Frank answered dutifully.

"We have a little situation here, Frank," Dugan continued.

"How can I help, sir?" Frank asked, beginning to relax in the hope that HE was not the "situation."

"Frank, we've just been informed that Mr. Holmes, president of Mr. Bodyparts, no longer is interested in performing his philanthropic services to the medical community. There is no doubt that this will set back the goals of medical science and will have an adverse effect on the mission of many of the companies we represent. We have a two-fold purpose here, Frank," Dugan continued. "First, we must find a replacement company to fill the needs of the medical community with good body parts for scientific research and study and, secondly, we must make sure that the confidentiality of our donors is kept in the highest regard. Do you follow me, Frank?"

"I think so, sir. What is it you'd like me to do?"

"Firstly, I understand that Holmes is planning to move. Find out when he is moving and where. You'll meet him on Friday night at the same place. Invite him for a drink, dinner, sleep with him if you have to, but get that information. Once you have it, call this number and just say where he's moving. Then hang up.

"Secondly, get packed between now and Friday. Load the trunk of the car with your clothing and personal items like family photos, the family Bible, that kind of stuff. Don't worry about anything you can buy and replace. Just leave everything. When you and your wife leave on Friday, you're not going back. We'll take care of closing down the apartment so don't worry about it and don't go back there. Ever.

"You go to Atlantic City, meet Holmes, do what you're supposed to, have a great time, stay until Sunday. A little bonus for the two of you," Dugan continued. "Then, get in the car bright and early on Sunday and drive to Bethesda, Maryland. The directions and address of your new home and new office are enclosed. I hope you like the place, Frank. We used an award-winning decorator to furnish the place," Dugan beamed.

"Then, on Monday," Dugan continued," follow the directions in the envelope to your new office. And call me when you get there from this cellular phone. Do not call me from any of the phones in your new office, ever. Do you understand, Frank?" Dugan asked, leaning forward toward Frank from the corner of his desk where he was perched.

"Yes, sir! You can count on me, sir," Frank replied.

"Good!" Dugan answered. "At the appropriate time, you'll be invited back to town for a meeting or two. We're saving you for a special job and we want you on the sidelines until then. You got it?"

Truth be known, Frank didn't understand at all. What the hell was going on and why was he going into exile? Frank wondered. But he was smart enough not to question a thing. After all, he was getting away from Maisy's family, moving into a decorator-furnished apartment, and moving on in the world. Didn't sound bad, at all, Frank thought, "At least I'm not leaving in that pine box."

CHAPTER TWENTY-SIX

MELANIE LEFT HER house at ten-fifteen, Thursday morning, leaving her driveway with directions in hand to Miriam Posner's house. She drove east and made the appropriate lefts and rights, meandering through the heavily treed streets and lanes until she came to the end of the instructions.

There stood a large, sweeping contemporary house planked with blond wood. The vaulting roof line boasted multiple skylights and three chimneys. The house was both angular and rounded, with terraces coming off of the living room and upper bedrooms. The round pipe railings gave the house the look of a ship.

Melanie pulled into the never-ending shrub lined driveway and parked in the circular drive in front of the entrance to the house. The bluestones crunched under the tires as she came to a halt. Before Melanie was out of her car, Miriam Posner opened the front door and called a cheery, "Welcome, my dear," to Melanie.

"Hello, I'm Melanie Cohen."

"Yes, dear. And you are the image of your father. Good thing he was a handsome fellow," Miriam chuckled.

Miriam was definitely one of Melanie's father's contemporaries. She had steel gray hair, bright blue eyes, and a slim figure. She wore an ice blue caftan and that hung loosely from the underarms in a tent shape. It was made in two layers, the bottom in polished cotton and the top layer in rayon chiffon. She reminded Melanie of the fairy godmother in fairytales of her childhood.

Miriam was a gracious hostess. She invited Melanie into the living room where she had coffee, tea, a platter of fruit, cheeses, crackers and morning biscuits beautifully arranged on a huge Rosenthal platter. The serving pieces complimented the contemporary house.

Melanie would never have guessed that Miriam would live in a house that looked like this. She seemed out of place in this thoroughly modern setting. But it was clear that this silver haired woman was not slowed down from keeping up with the times by her aging body.

The living room walls shot up twenty-two feet and were covered with silver foil wallpaper in a bamboo design. It was dazzling in the morning sunlight. The glow emanating from behind Miriam and her blue caftan radiated about her and gave her the look of an angel. Her sweet smile and gracious manner added to the serenity of the scene.

"So, dear, what keeps you busy?" Miriam pried.

"Well, the thing I'm most involved in is managing the foundation I've set up," Melanie answered.

"Well, that must keep you running about."

"In fact, it does. Lots of trips to New York City that I find exhausting so I set up a small office there and I stay over so I don't have to run back and forth so much," Melanie explained.

"What part of the city did you set your office up in, dear?'

"Actually, I took a small suite at The Algonquin. That way I've got my office space and my sleeping accommodations all organized in one spot at one fee. Worksout really well. I leave a few things there so I don't need to pack much and, if I decide to stay in at the spur of the moment, I have what I need to get by," Melanie explained. "If you're ever in the city when I'm there, you must come and visit! My suite is two stories high with twenty foot high windows and a terrace with spectacular views of the city!"

"Oh, is that where you were yesterday?" Miriam continued.

"Actually, yes. That's why I couldn't meet with you. But I'm usually in the city once, sometimes twice, a week. I just don't always stay overnight," Melanie concluded.

Wanting to change the subject, Melanie said, "What a wonderful house!"

"Well, it's nothing compared to the estate you were raised on, Melanie, but it's home. We have five acres and the gardens are lovely. If you are truly interested in flowers, I'll be happy to show them to you," Miriam went on.

"Oh, so you know why I' m here," Melanie replied.

"No, dear, I don't."

Melanie went into her explanation about the beauty of the sanctuary being compromised by the plastic greenery on the altar and her plans to overhaul the look at her own expense and effort. As she spoke, Melanie was amazed at the way the look of Miriam Posner's face changed from soft sweetness to hard as nails, and how her body moved from comfortably relaxed to military alert. It was clear that the warmth in the room was being replaced with a chill. Nonetheless, the obvious changes in the emotional temperature did not stop Melanie from telling her story.

When she finished, she waited for Miriam to reply. There was a long silence while Miriam drank some coffee and bit into a biscuit.

Finally, Miriam said, "As I mentioned to you, I have quite a garden. As a matter of fact, I have entered my roses and my orchids, which I grow in my greenhouse, in contests and I am proud to say I have won at least one award every year for the last twenty years. I have, in fact, considered placing some of my potted plants in the planter you refer to in the sanctuary but, for a variety of reasons, have not done so.

"At this time, however, the temple is looking into the matter of signing on an official caterer. We expect the contract to be signed before the year is over. The caterer will be building a new kitchen, a new social hall, and will be paying for some modifications to the sanctuary as part of getting the exclusive catering contract here. So it would be silly to make these changes, go to the expense and the trouble, when its all going to be changed when the new caterer gets settled in," Miriam concluded.

"But, according to what you're telling me, it will be months before the new caterer is in place and it could be months after that until all of these changes are implemented. I don't mind doing whatever it takes to get fresh flowers in there now, through the High Holy Days and right through to the day the new caterer is ready to do whatever it is to the sanctuary," Melanie protested.

"Well, that would just be wasteful and foolish, dear," Miriam responded.

"That doesn't make any sense," Melanie blurted out, not realizing she had spoken the words she was thinking.

Miriam responded, "Some things are just not your business, dear."

And then Melanie realized why she shied away from temple committees, temple boards, and temple projects. Somewhere between good ideas and good works, little minds and powerless people crawled in to take control and make decisions which don't have to be right, or just, or sensible. It only had to be their decision in their little corner of the world. For one moment in time, Miriam had control over something other than her roses and orchids in her garden. It was too bad that it was Melanie's good idea that got in the way.

With amazing graciousness, given her state of mind, Melanie thanked Miriam for making the time for her to visit her lovely home. Melanie left quickly, sending bits of gravel flying in her wake as she exited the long driveway.

Never again will I volunteer to do anything, Melanie vowed. Like Miriam, she, too, was used to getting her way.

But while Melanie did not get what she wanted, Miriam was given an unexpected treasure. Melanie keeps a suite at The Algonquin. What a juicy tidbit that was. Just this week, Miriam learned that David King and Allison Shapiro had a tryst at the Algonquin. Old Mrs. Benjamin had told her that Melanie had come by recently to help Allison out on the Oneg Committee. And David King had sent Melanie here to talk to her about flowers for the altar, of all things. Well, now, Miriam thought. There's your connection. Melanie is the one making the whole wretched thing possible by letting David and Allison use her suite at The Algonquin. She's as mean-spirited as her father was. It's all Melanie's fault that that marriage is falling apart, Miriam theorized, as she lifted the telephone to share this new information with her closest friends.

As Melanie sped away from the Posner mansion, the glare on the windshield made her notice how brightly the sun was shining. The sky was powder blue. It was a glorious day to be alive. Melanie bounced through the remaining errands on her list for the day: stop at the cleaners, return library books and get new ones, drop shoes at the shoe repair shop, pick up a few bunches of Shasta daisies at the florist, pick up milk, eggs, and ice cream, get a haircut and head home.

Having completed every item on her list, Melanie headed home.

As she turned the corner, she saw them: the dreaded interlopers; the feared family; "The Blacks."

"Those poor people," Melanie thought. "They haven't got a chance."

She wondered if they had any idea of the percolating hostility in the neighborhood. Under normal circumstances, Melanie would have continued, uninterruptedly, with her own plans. But, knowing what was brewing among her neighbors, Melanie felt compelled to stop to say hello and welcome the family.

"If the rumblings reach their ears, they'll know that there is at least one person in the area who hasn't prejudged them and has no agenda to make them miserable or make them evaporate," Melanie thought.

Melanie slowed down and parked in front of the construction site that would soon be their new house. "Hi there," she yelled to the threesome standing on the dusty mound destined to be their front lawn. "I'm Melanie Cohen. I live around the corner. I think we're going to be neighbors."

"Well, it sure looks that way," came the response from the tall muscular man. "I'm Trevor Winston and this is Trevor, Jr.," he beamed with pride as he made his introductions standing on his land in front of his new house-in-progress. "And this is my wife."

Her name was Rose and it suited her well. When she smiled, a radiance spread across her face like a blossom opening. Rose had spent her married life tending to her now seven year old son and her husband with the fervor of a guardian angel and rejoiced over their good deeds and accomplishments as evidence of her nurturing skills and capabilities of providing the fertile environment for their growth. She was a dignified woman, committed to her home, her family, and her church. She was a loving, compassionate person. In short, Rose had a history of being a good friend and a good neighbor. But she and her loved ones were not welcome in this neighborhood.

Melanie and the Winstons made small talk about the joys of watching a new home grow through the stages of construction and the pains of moving in and settling down. Trevor was a school psychologist which allowed him to get home by 3:30pm, pick up Rose and Junior, to come out to see how the house was progressing before it got dark. It was at the point of being completed on the inside so they could move in any day now.

Melanie told them she hoped she'd see them soon, again welcomed them to the neighborhood, and excused herself to run before her ice cream melted.

CHAPTER TWENTY-SEVEN

MELANIE DRESSED HURRIEDLY and with anticipation of the excitement that her breakfast with David King would bring. She could feel the electricity in the air. Something was about to happen that would change the direction of her life. And David King was just the guy to do it.

Melanie pulled into the parking lot at the Village Diner at 7:20am. She entered the diner and scouted out the perfect table: not too close to the door, not too close to the kitchen, a table with plenty of sunlight. When she was done shopping for furniture, she sat down. At exactly 7:30 am, David King walked through the door and entered the diner as he entered all places: like he owned it.

They ordered coffee and orange juice. David came straight to the point.

"Let's not waste any time," he said. "Let me get right to the bottom line, Melanie. My company is ready for expansion. I'm ready for expansion. But I can't do it alone. You have every quality I'm looking for in someone to be a significant part of my business life. I need a right arm. If my instincts about you are right, I think you will wind up being not only my right arm but my right and left legs and half of my brain. I will pay you handsomely with bonuses built in at every plateau. I'm reaching for the stars and I know I can get there. But I can't do it alone. Are you ready to hitch your wagon to my shooting star?"

His enthusiasm alone exhausted Melanie. But who could say no to him? Of course she'd do it, whatever "it" was. But she couldn't let him know how knocked out she was by his offer.

"Well, that does sound fascinating but I would like to know more about exactly what you've got in mind for me," Melanie explained.

"That's hard to say because every day will be different and you're going to have to do whatever it takes. Some days you'll be organizing production, other days you'll be selling, and other days you'll be troubleshooting and just helping me nail people down. The big item is that I want to move the company to New York City because that's where the action is. You'll have to decide if you want to commute every day or if you'd rather live in town. That's up to you. But what we need to do is a business plan to meet my vision for the company and then go out and find the kind of capital to make it all happen. I believe that, with you at my side, we can do it."

Hearing David say "we" can do this and "we" can do that swept Melanie along in the tide he had carefully constructed. But the opportunity to build a dream into a reality with a man as exciting as David could not be overlooked. By 8:30am, Melanie had all her questions answered in a way that the only response she could possibly give David was, "It will be my pleasure to work with you, David. I've got a suite in NYC and all I have to do is lock the door on the Long Island house and off I go! When do I start?"

David leaned back against the upholstered booth seat, folded his arms across his chest, and said, "Darlin', you've already started."

"Well, in spirit only, David!" Melanie responded. "I need some time to organize my life!"

A start date was set to give Melanie a chance to wind up some loose ends. They decided that Melanie could start just as soon as she was ready but that sooner would be better than later. Melanie promised to do her best to wind up her life on Long Island and move her focus and attention to New York City, to David King, his company and his projects.

CHAPTER TWENTY-EIGHT

F OR ALLISON, FRIDAY morning started with all the joyous routine of the preparation for the arrival of the Sabbath. She bounced out of bed and rushed around the house getting everything organized in her home before she departed for her round of errands to pick up a challah and wine for the Sabbath Dinner for her family before going to the temple to prepare for the Oneg Shabbat that would follow services. Jennifer had been a little cranky this morning so Allison decided to take Jennifer with her on her shopping trip and to the temple. She gathered up Jen's portable playpen and her favorite toys and put them in the trunk of the car before running back into the house to put the finishing touches on the den and kitchen so that her house was in good order before venturing out.

Dave was running late this morning and was enjoying a conversation over Cheerios with Joshua who was wearing his favorite polo shirt with the lion on it.

The sun streamed in long beams of light across the kitchen and cast a heavenly look on the tranquil family scene.

"How could I even think of breaking up this beautiful family," Allison thought. "I just don't appreciate how much I have," she chastised herself.

"The bus is late, Mommy," Josh volunteered.

"Yes, I see that," Allison responded, thinking that she needed to stay on her tight Friday schedule too.

"I've got to get going, Dave. Where's Sylvie?"

"I hear the water running so I guess she must be in the shower," Dave responded. "But why don't you run along. I'll wait for the school bus with Josh and I'll wait for Sylvie to get done so I can leave her with Jen and take off."

"No, that would really slow you down, "Allison replied. "I was planning on taking Jen with me on my errands and to the temple this morning anyway, so if you'll just wait for Josh's bus with him that would work and just leave Sylvie a note that I've got Jen with me. That way you can get on with your day, too."

"Sounds good to me. Be careful. See ya later, Al, "Dave called as Allison dashed about moving things around, putting things away and gathering up what she needed before she left the house.

Breathlessly, Allison leaned over Joshua and, with Jennifer on one arm, kissed him on the forehead, reminded him to be a good boy, and brushed Dave's face with her lips saying "so long" in the same efficient movement. In a whirlwind turn, Allison was out the big Dutch colonial door and into her car. Before Josh could get from his chair at the kitchen table to the front door, Allison and Jennifer had turned the corner and were out of sight. Josh returned to the table to finish his cereal, saddened that he got to the door too late to wave goodbye to Mommy.

Everything seemed to happen at once. The phone rang and the school bus honked as it turned into the Shapiro's driveway. Dave ran for the phone, picked it up and turned to see Josh running out of the front door without his little backpack. Dave put the telephone receiver down on the kitchen counter without even saying hello to the caller, grabbed Josh's backpack and ran out of the front door waving it wildly at the bus driver to get her attention.

Josh took his sack from Dave and leaned back into the safety of the bus to avoid the embarrassment of giving his Dad a kiss in front of all the kids. Dave stood in the driveway and waved to Josh until the bus, following the same route Allison had taken, turned the corner and was out of sight. It wasn't until Dave was back in the house that he realized that he had left the phone off the hook in the kitchen with an unknown caller literally left hanging.

As he picked up the phone to say hello and see if anyone had the patience to still be there, Dave became aware of the voices engaged in conversation on the other end. He was about to hang up, realizing that it was a call between Sylvie and one of her international friends, when the names Allison and David caught his attention. It troubled Dave that Sylvie could be gossiping about him and his wife.

Holding his breath to maintain silence at his end, Dave listened to hear the content of the conversation. Of all the things that flashed through Dave's mind of what he could possibly hear Sylvie and her friend talking about, he never expected, imagined or guessed that the David whose name and activities were being coupled with his wife was some other David. Dave didn't have to worry about remembering to breathe quietly while eavesdropping. The breath and life seemed to have drained from his body. That tumbled and churned feeling of being caught up in a wave at the seashore grasped his body. His heart raced. His skin became cold and sweaty. He wanted to unzip his body, jump out of it, and run somewhere. But where? There was no place to go with this one.

So he did the only sensible thing to do. He sat down in the heavenly sunlight of his tranquil kitchen and tried to let some order settle into the disarray of his thoughts. The whole world changed in less than a minute. How could everything that was so right only moments ago be so wrong now.

The ache in Dave's stomach, the pounding in his chest, the thickening in his throat, and the numbness of his brain interacted with the surrealistic confused state of the man who woke up this morning thinking that the only problem he had was how to make more money this year than he did last year. As he looked up from the kitchen table and gazed at the sunlight, Dave was overcome with a sense of amazement.

"How could the sun still be shining," he thought. "Didn't God know the world had just come to an end?"

Dave's fingers began to cramp. Looking down, he realized he was still holding the phone in his hand. He stood up from the table, walked to the wall and replaced the telephone receiver in its cradle. Suddenly, the numbness left his body and the pain set in. Tears ran down Dave's face. Anger ran through him like a chill. Sadness, pain, and rage, all welled within him in one tornado of emotion. He rested his forehead on the wall next to the phone and was absorbed in the darkness of the belly of Jonah's whale.

Dave was fixed in that position when Sylvie entered the kitchen. Seeing Dave pinned against the wall, she knew at once that the click she heard on the phone was Dave hanging up.

Oh, God, she thought. What have I done?

But that thought evaporated quickly for here was her chance. She'd plotted and planned and fantasized, on so many occasions, stories that allowed her to be the heroine that Dave would come to love. Dave was injured and she administered the first aid that saved him and he loved her passionately for her heroic act. Dave made a fatal error at his office that cost him a fortune and Sylvie's banking family in France bailed him out with a loan. Dave fell ill and Sylvie sat at his bedside endlessly and selflessly caring for his every need and nursing him back to health. And every fantasized story ended with the miraculous disappearance of Allison and the entrance of Mrs. Sylvie Shapiro, wife of Dave Shapiro, mother of the two Shapiro children, not to mention the one on the way, and partner in Dave's comfortable material world.

But this story had a better element. All prior stories removed Allison in some bizarre way. She was killed in a car accident. She fell into a coma with no chance of recovery so divorce became acceptable. She contracted a deadly disease that worked swiftly. And Sylvie was always the heiress apparent to pick up the pieces of the demise of the tragic exit of Allison. But that always made Allison a martyr. Everyone always felt sorry for Allison in those fairytales.

But not this time. Truth was so much better than Sylvie's fictions. Now Allison would be the devil, the outcast, the bad one. And Sylvie would be the sweet young thing who held down the fort, cared lovingly for the children, supported and cared for Dave, and pushed Allison out of her house, her community, and her life. Sylvie came up behind Dave and put her hand on his shoulder. Dave turned and looked into Sylvie's eyes. Dave's face reflected the torture he felt. Sylvie reached up and slowly put her hands on his face, cradling his tearstained cheeks.

"I'm so sorry," she said. "I didn't want you to learn about this. Not this way." Dave slid his hands around her and she clung to him embracing him tightly. Dave needed comforting and Sylvie performed on cue.

They stood, locked in the embrace that they both wanted to last forever so that neither of them would have to deal with the realities of their own lives and of the world outside of that embrace.

Dave followed the script that Sylvie had written for him. He responded to her gentleness and understanding caresses just as she had hoped, had schemed, had desired. It didn't take long for the two consenting adults to make their way to Sylvie's as yet unmade bed where one world ended and another began on a bright, sunshiny day.

CHAPTER TWENTY-NINE

ALLISON DROVE THROUGH as many drive-up windows as possible to avoid taking Jen in and out of the car. She drove through the banking window, the video return, the library book return and planned to drive through the dairy store drive-up lane to buy all the items she could that wouldn't spoil while they were in the car. Then she decided that would mean a second trip back later to pick up all the dairy products plus she still needed to go to the dry cleaners and run into two other shops that didn't have drive-up windows. Trying to take Jen in and out of all these places just made the baby cranky and wore Allison out.

"I think Mommy needs to take you home now to Sylvie, Jen. Did you have fun in the car with Mommy?" Allison asked, looking forward to the day when she would get a coherent response.

As she pulled into the driveway of her home, Allison started to tell Jen her plan to drop her off and run over to the temple and be back before Josh got home, but a quick look in the back seat revealed a snoozing child. Allison gathered up the bundles leaving Jen in her car seat to be removed last, lest she awaken her now.

She carried in all the sacks and packages and put them on the kitchen counters. Not seeing Sylvie anywhere on the first floor of the house, Allison assumed that Sylvie was well along in straightening the bedrooms. Allison hastily went out to the car to get the sleeping baby lest she awaken alone and frightened in the car.

Kicking the front door shut with her left foot as she entered the house, Allison quietly walked up the carpeted steps to the second floor where the bedrooms and Jen's nursery were located, trying her best not to jolt Jen out of her napping state. As she walked down the upstairs hallway, Allison's attention was drawn to unusual sounds coming from Sylvie's bedroom.

It took some time for the reality of the sight before her to make sense. Her first step at rationalizing the situation was to wonder which one was giving the other CPR.

Surely this could not be what she thought it was. But there was no evading the obvious. Standing in the doorway of Sylvie's room, with Jennifer asleep in her arms, Allison watched her world come thrusting to an end in a sun drenched hallway on a beautiful *erev* Sabbath morning. Realizing the magnitude and meaning of the scene before her, Allison searched her brain for something cool and sophisticated to say to project her image of being in control but all she could say was, "When you're through, you'll find me in the kitchen with my head in the oven."

Allison took the baby to her room and, with a gentle, loving motion, placed her in the crib and slid her hands out from under the sleeping child. The tears that ran down her face fell on the white "ducky "stretch suit that Jen was wearing. The irony was not lost on Allison. The days that would follow would not be easy like water running off a duck's back.

Allison went down to the kitchen. She could hear the water running in different parts of the house coming from the two upstairs bathrooms. She imagined Dave in one and Sylvie in the other, each trying to shower off their guilt and sins. She picked up the telephone and called Melanie. She was in no condition to deal with preparations for the Oneg today.

When Melanie heard the shakiness of Allison's voice, she knew better than to ask for explanations of why Alli couldn't take care of things. It was clear that Allison had a problem and Melanie didn't have the heart to add to Alli's problems even though she had no idea what those problems were.

As soon as Melanie assured her that she could be counted on, Allison moved on to the next call, not even taking the time to say goodbye.

The next call was to Dawn, Dave's sister. Allison wasn't sure whether she called her for comfort and support or to tell her what a rat-bastard her brother was. While she was dialing Dawn's number, Allison was a pillar of strength. But her strength melted the instant Dawn said, "Hello."

The sobs from Allison made it impossible for Dawn to identify who the devastated caller was.

"Sarah? Amy? Who is this? Judith is that you?" she continued guessing. It hurt Allison even more to know that she was not at the top of Dawn's "List of Those to be Concerned About."

"Dawn, it's me. Allison," she sobbed.

"My God. Is Dave all right? How are the kids? What's going on?" she interrogated.

Talk about pouring salt in a wound, Allison thought. I'm the hysterical one and her only questions are about Dave and the kids. Maybe I called the wrong person. Maybe I should just hang up.

"You're brother is screwing our nanny. Otherwise, everything's fine. Thanks for giving a shit!" And with that, Allison hung up the phone and reaffirmed for herself that no one really cared about her, anyway.

"Allison! Allison!" Dawn screamed into the phone. But Allison was gone. Dawn called back at once.

Dave had emerged from the bathroom and was hastily putting on his clothes when the phone rang. He grabbed it but before he could say a word, Dawn screamed, "What the hell is going on over there." Dave couldn't decide if the house was bugged or Dawn was psychic.

"What do you mean?" Dave asked.

"What are you doing home? Why aren't you at the office? Are you screwing Sylvie?"

Dawn asked all three questions with the same tone and matter-of-fact quality as if they all carried equal weight.

"It's not quite that simple," Dave replied.

"Seems simple enough to me! What's going on over there?"

"I need to talk to you, Dawn. I'll come over, okay?"

"Of course it's okay," she said with a tone that conveyed that protective "you're my handsome brother who can do no wrong" quality.

"I'll be there as soon as I can," he replied, responding to her supportive tone.

As he passed Sylvie's room, he saw that she was standing in her doorway with her suitcase in her hand.

"Please drop me at Adriana's house. I'm sure they'll let me stay there while I figure out what I will do now."

"Well, you're right about not staying here. Come with me and I'll drop you wherever you want."

Dave and Sylvie ran down the steps and out to Dave's car. Neither said a word to Allison. Allison sat, feeling like a stranger in her own house, in her sun drenched kitchen on a beautiful Friday morning, numb to the joy of the approaching Sabbath and feeling lost and alone.

Allison caught her balance and decided she was not living her own fantasy about what a swell suburban life she was living and what a peachy guy Dave was. She decided there wasn't a thing about her house she liked and the very walls seemed to be crushing in on her like the entry foyer to the Haunted House at Disney World. There was no question in her mind that she had to follow Sylvie's example and get out of the house with a guy who showed interest in her. So she made the move that would change the course of her personal history.

Allison picked up the telephone and called David King. And then she started packing. Using Jen's naptime to her advantage, Allison was able to get everything she needed to do done by the time Josh got off the nursery school bus. Allison had packed every item of clothing owned by the three of them and all of the favorite toys and books of each of them and put them in her car and on her roof rack. She then drove to the address David King had given her and raced into his arms and the new life he had promised her.

Allison, David, and the children spent their first Shabbat dinner together. Allison felt empty and confused. This was not the way this day was supposed to end. This was not the way she and David were supposed to begin.

Things couldn't have gone any more wrong.

CHAPTER THIRTY

"THINGS COULDN'T HAVE gone any more wrong today," Melanie muttered to herself, as she rushed about trying to get everything accomplished at the Temple and still have time to attend to her personal list of errands. As she went about her day's tasks, she was constantly reminded that the time-crunch she was feeling was the direct result of Allison's breathless phone call this morning.

What could have happened that made Allison sound that way, Melanie wondered.

Nonetheless, even with the extra things that got dumped on her, Melanie was on track and knew she would get everything accomplished in order to be at services on time.

"Things couldn't have gone any more wrong today," Dave said as he entered Dawn's house.

He towered over his sister making it convenient for him to kiss the top of her head. Dawn ushered her baby brother into the den with all the loving concern due an occasion such as this. She tried to hide her rage at the idea that he and the au pair were having a go at it. She knew she would have to show only concern for Dave in order to get the whole story. If she acted like a judgmental parent he might just walk out without telling her what was going on so she would have to stay cool but caring.

After hearing his story, Dawn sat in complete shock. She was shocked that Allison could have been anything but a faithful and dutiful wife . . . but not completely surprised because Dawn always thought she was not worthy of Dave. She was shocked that David King was interested in Allison . . . why would he want her when he could have had anybody?

She was shocked that the au pair knew all the details while Dawn was just finding out. But she understood how such news would have sent baby brother Dave over the edge and into the arms of a lovely, young French woman to soothe his pain. After all, Dave was human.

So Dawn invited Dave to stay for Shabbat dinner with her family and to go to Temple with them that night. Dave decided that staying for dinner was a good idea. After all, he had to eat.

But he wasn't ready to face the community just yet so he'd stay at home, her home, and unwind, maybe even spend the night since he wasn't quite ready to go home and face Allison. Dawn bought that and they all went about their preparations for the approach of sundown.

As the sun set at 6:14pm, matches were being struck all over the east coast in one simultaneous movement and were held against the wicks of tall candles. Families participated in the blessings to usher in the Sabbath with light, with wine, with golden braided ceremonial bread, rich with eggs and milk. Blessings were bestowed by the parents on the children. Wishes for a Good Sabbath were placed with kisses on the cheeks of each family member from every other family member and a wonderful meal that had been in preparation most of the afternoon was served, consumed and enjoyed by all.

Tables were quickly cleared and families gathered by the front door of their homes to exit and make their way to Temple. This week, Allison and Dave would not participate in this ritual as a family and neither of them would go to Temple.

With all that was going on in her family, Dawn managed to find the time to do a little "research" into the news she learned today. It didn't take too many telephone calls to find out what most of the community already knew. One more shock was visited upon Dawn when she learned that Melanie Cohen had seen Allison and David King in the lobby of a hotel in New York City and had brought that news back to the community to damage the reputations of her brother and sister-in-law.

That wicked bitch, Dawn thought. The rich witch who drives around in a Rolls Royce daddy left her thinks she can just spread gossip about anybody and get away with it. I'll fix that, Dawn decided as she slid into the jacket of her suit and made her way down the driveway to the family car and her impatient husband.

Once inside, she brought him up-to-date on the gruesome details of the afternoon's events.

The traffic was backed up for a block in each direction of the entrance to the parking lot of the temple. Cars pulled in and filled spots quickly in the lot and, correspondingly, their passengers filled the seats in the sanctuary. Congregants greeted each other with "Gut Shabbos," handshakes and kisses while they stood near their seats and in the aisles catching up on the what was new since last week.

Dawn's telephone calls around town were as much informative as they were an inquiry. Starting with, "What do you know about a relationship between Allison Shapiro and David King?"

If the recipient of the call knew nothing beforehand, she certainly had a good idea when Dawn hung up. As a result, the entrance of Dawn into the sanctuary created an instant buzz followed by an artificial silence created by multiple individuals cueing others to hush.

Melanie slipped into the sanctuary only moments before the Friday night service was to start although she had been in the Temple for more than an hour readying the coffee and putting out the flowers and trays of bakery items that had arrived since her midday departure. As she scanned the sanctuary looking for a seat, she spotted one on the far side of the center aisle. It was the same seat she occupied on the day her cousin Maisy married Frank. She thought about them as she settled herself into her seat. They had been close as children but all that changed when her family moved miles away. She wondered how ditzy Maisy and dour Frank were doing. She hadn't heard from them since their wedding. Not even an acknowledgement of the pair of beautiful lead crystal Tiffany candlesticks she had sent them to symbolically fill their lives with joy and light.

It's a good thing Tiffany's has a great tracking system or I'd never even know they were delivered, Melanie thought. She continued to wonder how Frank and Maisy were doing until a few moments later when the rabbi appeared at the pulpit and silence fell over the group.

The rabbi's impish face beamed his enjoyment and appreciation of the radiance of the Sabbath. Every bit of his round body reflected the glow of the candles on the bema and the glow he felt from the celebration of the end of another week and the twenty-four hours that would now be set aside for spiritual replenishment to take on the new week ahead. He stepped down from the bema to stand in the aisle and say the Kaddish with a family of mourners. He performed a baby naming for a beautiful young couple attending with their infant daughter. He led the congregation in rejoicing the impending Bar Mitzvah of two young men and the Bat Mitzvah of a young women, all thirteen years old and ready to take their places in the Jewish community as adult members of the congregation.

"The girl looks like an adult, I'll admit to you," Miriam Posner whispered to the woman on her right. "She looks like she's twenty. But those two little boys don't look like their ready for much!" she chuckled.

The rabbi read from the prayer book. The cantor chanted. The congregation rose and sat on cue. And a member of the Ritual Committee bestowed the appropriate gifts from the congregation on all those celebrating a special occasion this Shabbos.

And then it came time for the sermon. Always filled with conviction. Always stirring. Usually controversial. This week was no exception.

If the Shapiro family thought it had its problems, it was nothing compared to what was going on with the Ginzbergs. Mel Ginzberg.

Now that was an anomaly if ever there was one. He was short, slim, dark haired and well groomed. No, immaculately groomed. His secret idol was David King. But he wasn't even a close second, try as he did. He held an impressive appointed position in county government and acted like he had been installed in his job by Devine intervention. He was haughty, aloof, and acted as though allowing you to shake his hand should be considered an honor. He was, therefore, elected President of the Temple Brotherhood twice and served on the Temple board for more years than anyone could remember.

It was, therefore, with a certain amount of delight that many members of the congregation discussed the recent stories in Newsday regarding Mel's arrest for trying to force a go-go dancer at a club in a nearby town into his car at midnight at gunpoint! Who could believe that of scrawny, holier-than-thou Mel? While there were those who said the story could not possibly be true, follow up stories corroborated all of the hideous details to the humiliation of his wife, children, county government, and the congregation. Once the story hit the news, the calls flooded the rabbi's office. And it was this fact that was the foundation for the sermon this Friday night.

When the rabbi began with," I am quite disgusted with the events of this week," most people in the congregation assumed that his disgust was with Mel. But that was not so.

"What Mel did, Mel did. Who knows what he could have been thinking . . . or drinking, for that matter, that prompted him to do something so out of character to the man we know," the rabbi began. "Only he is responsible for his actions and only he is accountable to the law of the land and the Laws we live by," Rabbi continued.

"But what about all of you? What about all of you who called this week to ask me, 'So, Rabbi, did you hear about Mel? So, Rabbi, how about Mel Ginzberg? So, Rabbi, what do you think about Mel now and how do we expunge him from the Temple board?' You're going to find this hard to believe, people. But it's not Mel I'm upset with!"

There was an audible gasp in the sanctuary.

"It's all of you I'm upset with!" the rabbi continued. "Mel did an incredibly dumb thing. But it's not my job to judge him. And it's not your job either! So what is your job? Your job is to understand that a member of this congregation is at a very dark time in his life and it's a very dark time for his family as well. The Ginzberg family has given selflessly of their time and their contributions to this temple in terms of their efforts to make it possible for you to sit in this comfortable and beautiful sanctuary tonight. They don't need you to add to their problems with your gossip, your judgments, and your gloating over their misfortune no matter how their misfortune befell them. What they need now is to know that you will circle the wagons around their family and protect them in the one place on earth where they should be able to enter with peace and love. I am ashamed of all of the calls and the callers I heard from, and there were hundreds. I am ashamed that some of you stood in this sanctuary tonight before the service and started the Sabbath by giving energy and momentum to destroying a family that is a member of your congregation."

The rabbi's attention was distracted by Marvin Finster who leaned over to whisper in his wife's ear.

"Do you have something to say, Marvin?" the rabbi asked.

"Yeah," Marvin answered. "I didn't come here tonight to listen to this."

"Then you can leave Marvin because nobody's going to tell me what to say from my pulpit."

The absence of sound in a room filled with two hundred people is eerie. Not a creature was stirring. No one dared to move. Not even Marvin and his rotund wife, Rhoda, who at that moment wished she had never married him.

The service concluded with the singing of Adonalum. The rabbi exited the bema through a side door that led directly into his office where he would meet with the Bar and Bat Mitzvah families for a few private minutes to congratulate them on living to see this glorious occasion and would explain why their children were lucky to have a sermon of this nature on the eve of their entry into the adult spiritual community.

The congregants were relieved to rise and file out into the Social Hall for the Oneg Shabbat. Long tables with navy blue skirts bordered two walls of the room. They were covered with cakes and cookie platters wrapped in colorful cellophane wrap that Sisterhood board members were busily removing. On the center table were wine and challah and coffee, juices and sodas were off to the side. The older children found one another quickly at the cookie table while the younger ones tugged on their parents' hands begging to go home to sleep.

Melanie emerged from the kitchen carrying two pitchers with non-dairy liquid creamer to put on the coffee table. Her obligations to the Oneg, which she promised Allison she would fulfill, were now officially completed. She could now enjoy the Oneg and the fruits of her labors.

With a thimble-sized paper cup filled with kosher wine in hand, Melanie stopped by groups of three, four, six people at a time to say Gut Shabbos. She smiled her usual "glad to see you" smile. But after a few minutes of standing with each group she moved on to the next.

At first, Melanie thought she was just coming in at a bad time in the conversation. But after dropping in on ten different little clusters of congregants who were smiling and chatting with cake in one hand and coffee or wine in the other, and finding that the conversation almost stopped at the sight of her, or the conversation never stopped long enough to include her, Melanie began to feel a sense of paranoia that something was wrong and it was she! Not willing to give into her ridiculous observations, Melanie moved on to a group of six people standing against the moveable wall that divided the Sanctuary from the Social Hall. She knew the Schwartzes and the Rosenthals well and she knew Dawn from casual conversations at temple functions. Dawn's husband she knew only by sight. As she approached the group everyone was cordial and friendly except Dawn whose coldness didn't make sense to Melanie.

Melanie's interaction in the conversation was met by snide comebacks by Dawn that shocked Melanie who couldn't understand why Dawn was being so nasty to her. Melanie finally had had enough of Dawn's unpleasantness and said good night to the group indicating it had been a long day and she was going home now.

Melanie carried the vision of Dawn's twisted face with her as she went to the coatroom to pick up her jacket. As she entered the cavernous area filled with outer wraps, she noticed three women enmeshed in the garments, chatting intently. When they noticed Melanie, one of the three beckoned to Melanie to join them.

"Hey, Mel. Gut Shabbos. We were just talking about Allison. It's just terrible, isn't it?"

"What's happened?" Melanie asked. "I knew something was wrong this morning when she called me to pitch in for her with the Oneg chores but she didn't tell me what was going . . ."

Anxious to tell the tale, one of them interrupted her and said," Allison is having an affair with David King. Somebody in the congregation saw her in the lobby of a hotel in New York City and told some people who told some people until it got back to Dave, her husband, and today they split up."

"Oh, that *is* terrible!" Melanie gasped. "They were such a perfect couple."

"Yeah, well, I've always been suspicious of the saintly types."

"What a shame," Mel continued in her own train of thought. "No wonder she was breathless when she called me."

Melanie slipped into her jacket and walked out of the coatroom, out of the lobby of the temple and out into the cold night air. This chill of the evening could not compare to the chilling news she had just received. She was so sorry her evening ended with those three women in the coatroom.

They really messed up my glow, Melanie thought as she drove through the dark, winding streets to her home.

CHAPTER THIRTY-ONE

ALLISON TURNED OFF of Northern State Parkway onto the service road following David's instructions carefully. After several lefts and rights, she entered the grounds of The Seasons. The sign said, "A Luxury Village for Fine Living," under the main title. Twenty-five feet down the entry road, there was a signpost directing traffic to four different buildings along four different paths.

Autumn, Winter, and Spring split off to the left and straight ahead. Allison was destined for Summer. Taking the right fork, the irony of the name of the building which was to become her new home, and a new beginning filled with the warmth and sunlight of a summer day, did not escape her.

When she pulled up in front of the building, she was met by the doorman, the car valet, and David King. Before anyone else could reach the driver's side of the car, David was there opening the door and sweeping Allison up and out from behind the wheel. In one unbroken movement, Allison was on her feet and in David's arms. There is no safer place in the world than in David's arms, Allison thought. I am so lucky to have him in my life.

A woman in a royal blue and white gingham check maid's uniform, complete with a little white circular apron and cap, appeared on the scene to help with the personal items. Allison and David walked ahead to the elevator carrying nothing while a parade of buildings and grounds personnel, the maid, and a Mary Poppins style nanny, complete with hair in a bun, organized the movement of the baggage and children to the sixteenth floor apartment.

Allison was numb. All of the sights and sounds she was exposed to were being seen and heard through marshmallows and cotton puffs. Everything was surreal. Everything except David's gentle touch and the scent of Santos de Cartier that enveloped him.

The elevator doors opened. David, Allison, Jen, Josh and the nanny and the maid stepped off onto the sixteenth floor. Allison took David's lead and followed him down the hallway to the door marked, "The July Penthouse." If the scene at her home with Dave this morning could be described as explosive, then David was ending her day and beginning her life with fireworks.

In his always flamboyant style, David opened the door to the suite and stepped out of the way so that Allison could absorb the full impact of the interior and the view that lay beyond the panoramic expanse of windows.

Allison gasped. It was only on the pages of Architectural Digest that she had seen rooms that looked like these. As she and David stepped into the living room/dining room area, David quietly instructed the maid and the nanny to take the children to their rooms. Allison continued on in her bewildered state.

The rectangular room before her was enormous. The wall she faced was constructed from a series of five ten-foot long sliding glass doors that opened onto a balcony running the entire length of the room. Both of the walls at the far right and far left of the room had fireplaces. The one at the right was faced with Westchester gray stone placed in large hand cut pieces that created a snug jigsaw puzzle design. The wall at the left was faced in pearl gray marble squares swirled with white. The carpet was silver gray and the furnishings were all upholstered in gray velvet with throw pillows and accents in navy blue and yellow.

"I had it all done in gray for you so you can pick any color you want and the room will take on the flavor of the moment," David whispered.

"I'm in shock," was all that Allison could say.

"Then don't say anything until you're ready to," David replied.

As Allison walked around the penthouse, she discovered that the two interior fireplaces each served the room behind so that the master bedroom and the kitchen profited from the two dining room and living room fireplaces. The master bedroom had every feature one could wish for including a sunken tub. Marble and mirrors abounded. The best part was that the children's rooms and the master bedroom opened onto a penthouse garden area complete with redwood deck, children's swing set, sandbox, play equipment, and swimming pool.

"How did you do this so fast?" Allison asked with amazement.

"I didn't do it fast. It's been done and waiting for you for months. At least now I won't feel so bad about having paid the rent on a place that's not being used. I had hoped you and the children would have been here months ago. But that's okay. You're here now," David said.

"Yes, I'm here now. But what am I doing here?"

"You're doing the only thing that makes any sense. You're spending the rest of your life with me."

At that moment, Josh came running into the master bedroom with his arms filled with toys.

"Look, Mommy. Look what I found in the little boy's room. Trucks! Lots and lots of them. Can I play with them?"

"Absolutely," David replied. "They're for you. They're yours!"

"Wow," Josh exploded as he turned to run back to the treasure chest he had unearthed down the hall.

"I did what I thought you wanted, Allison. I took this place in your name and I paid the rent on it for twelve months in advance. Unfortunately, for about four of those months it's gone empty. I'll pay another four months next week so you'll have the full twelve months in front of you to feel comfortable that this is what you want before we go to the next level of our relationship.

"I'm not ready to talk about next levels today, David. I'm still getting used to the idea that we live here."

"We don't live here," David answered. "You live here . . . with the children. Once you are divorced and we are married, we can live here if we haven't already gotten a house organized for us to live in."

"You're amazing, David. Just amazing."

David walked Allison over to the center of the sliding glass wall. The sun was beginning to set and the sky was a blaze of orange light. The tree trunks looked like black velvet against the sky. And from the sixteenth floor of the Summer building, they could see the skyline of New York City. Allison felt so close to David in that moment. How wonderful it was to have someone who rescued her from the pit she had fallen into today. What a wonderful place to be, to live.

What a wonderful man to share it with. As he held her close to him she knew there was nowhere in the world as safe as in his arms. She knew she would never go back to where she had come from. She would never look back. The focus of her life would be straight ahead.

The maid announced that dinner was ready. The table was set for Shabbat dinner. As Allison surveyed all that was around her, she could only think of the Oneg she didn't prepare, the Shabbat dinner at her house with Dave that was unattended, the Friday night service she would not go to at the temple, the Bar Mitzvah and Baby Naming gifts David would not give tonight.

And with all that David was lovingly providing for her, she could not help but feel that this was not the way this day was supposed to end. This was not the way that she and David were supposed to begin.

Things couldn't have gone more wrong.

CHAPTER THIRTY-TWO

THE DAWNING OF the next day brought Melanie to her feet early. The sun streamed through her bedroom window with such intensity that the chrome and crystal knick-knacks reflected sparkles everywhere. It was impossible to continue to sleep in such brilliant light. As Melanie stirred, she decided to push herself out of bed and get a head start on the list of items that needed her attention, especially with her impending career move. She raced around the house, getting ready to meet the day and then jumped into her car.

As she turned the corner and entered the main street to her community, a moving van came into view. The van was parked in the driveway of the Winston's new home. Melanie felt compelled to stop to greet them and wish them well.

It wasn't Melanie's nature to become involved with her neighbors. She always assumed that the fact that those around her chose to live in the same community did not mean that they had anything else in common. She had a very full life that didn't include time for "coffee with the girls."

But, somehow, this was different. Melanie knew she would not have stopped to act as "the welcome committee" if this were just another lily-white family, of no particular description, moving in. She wasn't seeking a friendship or a relationship of any kind. She just felt compelled to make a statement, by her simple act of wishing the Winstons well, that there were people in the neighborhood who viewed their moving in with no ill-will. She hoped that the memories of her dropping by would be recalled by Rose and Trevor if, in fact, her other neighbors' ugly behavior reached the ears of the newcomers.

Melanie would have knocked before entering but the storm door was propped in a fully opened position and the front door was wide open to allow easy entry and exit for the movers. Melanie yelled hello from the doorway as she stepped inside.

Rose emerged from the kitchen holding a dishtowel in one hand and kitchen utensils in the other. She was wearing a red bandana-patterned shirt and navy chinos and looked like the perfect model for a poster for the moving company entitled, "Moving Day."

"Look what we have here!" Rose exclaimed with a million-dollar smile spreading across her face. "Our first visitor! Welcome and please come in. Be careful, though. There's barely an empty spot to put your feet down," Rose giggled, already overjoyed to share her moving day with a new neighbor.

"I saw the moving van and just thought I'd stop in to wish you lots of happiness in your new home. Please don't let me get in your way. I know you have a lot to do," Melanie said.

"Well, I'm just trying to get the kitchen under control!" Rose responded, cheerily. "It's next to impossible with Junior underfoot looking for snacks and juice every three seconds. I can't even find the boxes with the cups! But we're managing. I figure another hundred years and I'll have it together," she laughed.

Melanie liked Rose instantly. It was a pleasure to see her smiling face and experience her cordial charm under the trying circumstances of moving day. Rose's positive attitude triggered Melanie's appreciation of Rose's approach to life and made her wonder what Rose was like when things were more stabilized.

Melanie knew she wanted to know Rose better and decided to find a way to make her moving day less stressful and more memorable.

Instantly, Melanie had a plan.

"Tell you what, Rose," Melanie began, "let me get our of your way so you can make some headway."

"Well, do stop back again when we can really enjoy your company," Rose replied cheerfully, as Melanie hopped around boxes, cartons, and bundles, making her way to exit through the front door. Melanie already had plans to reappear at that door as dusk fell. Within hours, Melanie was back.

"Good Heavens! What do you have there?" Rose asked of Melanie as she reached the front door for the second time that day. "Let me turn on the porch light and help you. What in God's name have you got there?"

"Dinner!" was Melanie's one word response. "I figured you guys must be hungry by now and I don't think you're in the mood to sit in a restaurant right now so . . . here it is! I hope you like Swedish meatballs. It's one of my specialties," Melanie boasted.

Rose's smile spread across her face. Trevor set about clearing a spot to picnic in the kitchen. Melanie had thought of everything else: paper plates, plastic utensils, napkins, serving pieces, paper cups and some flowers for a centerpiece on the table they created from a shelf balanced on a can of spackle covered with a plastic red checkered tablecloth. It wasn't elegant but it did have its own unique charm. Plastic food storage bowls were opened to reveal salad, the main course, and dessert. Trevor couldn't stop talking about the lovely gesture and delicious food. Junior was just happy to eat. And Rose was consumed by the specialness of the outreach and the blessing she felt in having this kind and thoughtful neighbor.

The Winston family settled into the community. Trevor was a magician at landscaping and gardening and enjoyed the process of toiling in the earth. The Winston's property was whipped into shape quickly under his watchful eye. Trevor enjoyed retelling the story of some passerby stopping, shortly after they moved in, and asking him how much he charged for lawn care and landscaping.

"You should have seen his face when I said,' Well, shucks, sir, I don't charge nuthin'. I gets to sleep wid da lady of the house!"

"Oh, you go on," Rose would giggle with each of Trevor's retellings. "That's an awful story."

"Well, it's true," Trevor insisted.

"I don't believe you for a minute, Trevor Winston," Rose would say, swatting at him with her hand.

Rose, Trevor, and Trevor, Junior joined the local Lutheran Church. They were the only black family in the congregation. This wasn't a new experience for the Winstons. They had always lived in a white neighborhood and belonged to the local church. But this was a new experience for the neighbors and the congregants. Pastor Beaumont and the church members embraced them and the Winston family became active and integral members of the congregation. Trevor was an usher. Rose joined the Ladies Altar Guild and took delight in taking her turn at hand washing and ironing the Irish linens for the altar. Rose taught in the Sunday School where Junior was a student with a 100% attendance record. Rose saw to that.

The neighbors finally calmed down and realized their world, as they knew it, did not come to an end and disaster did not befall them with the entrance of the Winston family to the community. To the contrary, they were the kind of neighbors people wish for.

Over the next months, the Winston family did very well. Junior was doing extremely well. He was a serious student and the pride of his second grade teachers, both in the public school and at Sunday School. Thanks to Trevor Sr.'s coaching, Junior was the star of his soccer and Little League baseball teams. He had made lots of friends at school and had assimilated well into his new surroundings. Rose was very proud of her "Little Trev."

Trev developed a special friendship with a schoolmate named Randy Corbet. In a very short time, Trev and Randy had bonded. They enjoyed the same sports and enjoyed each other's companionship. They sought out one other at once on the playground, at recess, in the lunchroom, and as partners on line.

Rose walked Trev to the school bus every morning and waited for him every afternoon, greeting him with her big smile and a hand to hold the books that wouldn't fit in his schoolbag. Once home, Trev knew the routine: change clothes, have a snack, and settle down with homework before going out to play.

For Rose, life was perfect. She counted her blessings daily: she had her husband, who adored her, her precious son, her lovely home and her church to fill her days with meaning and love. And she had made friends in the new neighborhood, too. There were the churchwomen she met as a member of the Ladies' Altar Guild and the Sunday School teachers. She had also met some very nice people at PTA meetings. Life was very good.

And then there was Melanie, a unique individual Rose had grown to enjoy, admire, and respect, but not really understand. Why hadn't that clever, attractive and talented woman ever married? There must be a story to explain that, Rose thought.

Ash Wednesday started the Lenten period. Rose assisted Pastor Beaumont with the preparations for a Wednesday evening service that took place every week until Easter. Rose enjoyed these services because they were different from Sunday Mass. Each one left her with something that truly made her search her soul for answers to questions she never explored before.

On one of Melanie's afternoon visits, Rose invited her to come to a Wednesday night service. "It's not a 'preachy' thing," Rose explained. "It's more of a thought-provoking session that will lead you into the corners of your own life. Please come," Rose implored. "I know you'll get something of value from it."

"How can I turn down an offer like that?" Melanie responded. She promised Rose she would check her calendar and find the next Wednesday night that would work. As Melanie promised, she found a free Wednesday night on her calendar and planned to attend Rose's church service with her.

When the night arrived, Melanie and Rose climbed the twelve steps that led to the huge red double doors of St. Mark's Lutheran Church. It was an old historic church built in 1780 by the settlers of the town. It was small, with a stone exterior. The wooden floors were highly polished and reflected the lights and candles that brightened the church.

On the pews were cushions with colorful geometric needlepoint designs handmade by the women of the congregation. The stark simplicity of the building was warmed by the light and the loving touches one could feel within. The altar was covered by the crisply ironed Irish linen that Rose had labored over, and fresh flowers were placed around the altar.

Pastor Beaumont spoke about the introspective quality of Lent and then introduced a film called, "Three Archins of Land," for the congregation to watch and reflect upon. Melanie watched the film with fascination. It was an old film, produced in black and white. In it, a well-dressed man, wearing a suit and hat and carrying a briefcase, seemed to be being chased by something although the camera never seemed to catch a glimpse of what was after him. Fixated on the man, the camera showed him quicken his steps, begin to trot and, finally, break into a run. He panted louder and louder as his pace quickened and he began to lighten his burden, first by throwing away his briefcase and, then, by shedding his jacket, his tie and his shirt. He ran through the town and into the countryside. He ran until he could run no more from the off-camera demon that was chasing him. And, when he could run no more, he fell to the ground.

As he lay there, panting heavily, weary from the run and covered in perspiration, he finally could see the dangerous demon he had been running from full-face just before he died of exhaustion. And the demon was himself.

"So, for all his running," Rose said, stopping to reflect for a moment on the steps of the church, "all he got was three archins of land, a biblical measurement which equals six feet, the depth of a grave."

"I'm really glad you invited me, Rose," Melanie responded. "I really appreciated being here. Please invite me again."

"Oh, go on, girl!" Rose beamed with a giggle. "You're welcome anytime! Don't stand on ceremony. Just come along!"

Melanie enjoyed Rose's warm, open and positive approach to life. Rose's absolute faith in her religion, strange as it seemed, helped Melanie focus on the meaningfulness of her own religion in her life and prodded her curiosity to know and understands the origins of her own traditions and observances which she took so for granted.

Melanie did not want the evening to end abruptly. The film had evoked a feeling of turmoil within her. She just knew she would not be able to fall asleep quickly so she suggested to Rose that they stop at the Village Diner for coffee and cake, probably from her own experiences of religious services followed by "a little something to eat."

Rose checked her watch before accepting the invitation. "It is a school night, you know. I have to get up really early tomorrow to have Trev at school by 8:00am. They're having an early rehearsal of the school play. He has a lead part," she said with pride.

But with a little coaxing on Melanie's part and the persuasive argument, "How long could it take to have coffee and cake?" they were seated in the diner within five minutes.

The diner, the only one open twenty-four hours in a twenty mile radius, was always packed, regardless of the hour.

"It looks like the dinner hour rush in here!" Rose commented as they were seated at their booth. "I hope they serve us quickly. I can't be sluggish in the morning. Trev is so excited about this performance of his."

"You are incredible, Rose. No matter what you are doing, you never forget you are a mother first." Melanie's words touched Rose.

"Well, I had good training," Rose said, lowering her eyes, looking downward at her hands folded in her lap.

"Your mother must have been amazing," Melanie said with deep compassion as she noticed a tear trickle down Rose's face which was transformed by the emotional charge surging through her body.

"Oh, she was amazing, all right," Rose continued, lifted her face to make eye contact with Melanie. "She was amazing."

There was a tone in Rose's delivery that made it impossible to be sure of Rose's meaning.

"I'm not sure if I understand your message, Rose."

"Melanie," Rose began, speaking through pursed lips to hold back her tears and rising rage, "there are two ways to learn. You can learn from great examples and decide that is exactly what you want to do, or, you can learn from bad examples and decide that that is something you never want to do. I learned to be a good mother from bad examples," Rose continued, tears streaming down her face.

"The funny thing is that, if you met my mother, Miss Honeysuckle Rose, you would be completely charmed by her. She presents herself as the sweetest, nicest, most charming and lovely woman you would ever want to know. And I guess she is. But her wonderful graces never transcended into motherhood."

Melanie did not interrupt Rose as the outpouring gained momentum.

"I promised myself my child would come first. Always, in all things. I promised myself my child would always know he would be safe, secure, and loved. I promised myself that nothing I could prevent would ever harm my child. I learned from my mother's example exactly what I would never do." Rose stopped for a moment to catch her breath.

"You must have some awful childhood memories," Melanie interjected.

"Well, I could erase, excuse, rationalize and forgive all of that if my mother turned out to be a mother when I became an adult and married and Trev came along. But, unfortunately, I grew up but my mother never did. She's the same self-centered conceited woman she always was who thinks all is right with the world if she can look in the mirror and smile at what she sees."

Rose took a deep breath, readying herself to step into an area she rarely revisited. There were not many people with whom Rose would share her deepest wounds. But she trusted Melanie.

Sensing there was more Rose wanted to say, Melanie sat still and silent, allowing the coffee to get cold, not wanting to disturb Rose's outpouring even with the sounds of a cup touching down lightly on a saucer.

"There were just so many times, routinely, that my mother was just not there for me. Oh, she was home all the time, but she was just not there for ME. But of the encyclopedia of stories I could tell you from both my childhood and adulthood that would just blow you away, there is one moment that sickens me just in recalling it, so I put it in a box in the attic of my brain and filed it away. I could unzip my brain and bury it and never revisit it again, but I keep it so I will never forget to be a very different kind of mother. Some very bad memories have very positive effects. My whole growin' up was packed with just those kinds of experiences. But they helped me be who I am today so I am not ungrateful for the experience," Rose concluded.

Almost afraid to walk on Rose's pain, Melanie reflected on whether she should ask the question, "What was that memory locked in the attic?' and before she had finished thinking the words, Rose began to tell the story.

"My mother was thirty-four when my father passed on. I was seven. If you ask my mother, my father was the light of her life. They were high school sweethearts. Actually, she fell in love with him in Junior High but he didn't know she was alive yet. His body wasn't cold, thirty days later, when she began to date."

She met this guy. He was good lookin', charming, nice enough, and she went out with him for about six weeks when he had to take a business trip. He was gone about two days when he called. Mind you, this is now less than three months after my father passed on. And after cooing on the phone for a bit, my mother calls me away from the kitchen table where I was doing my homework, holds the phone out to me and says, "Carl is on the phone. Say 'Hello, Daddy.' *Say, 'Hello, Daddy.' What could she have been thinking*," Rose implored, tears flowing down her face. "Well," she continued, "we *know* what she was thinking."

Melanie and Rose chuckled at the "nothing to laugh about" story. "Can you imagine how I felt? I was paralyzed! My throat felt like somebody stuck a log in it! I felt dirty all over. I put my hands up in the air as she pushed the phone at me again and I definitely said, "NO!" But I was this good little girl taught to obey my mama and here she was again with this phone telling me, 'Do as I say, child!' I think, if I had been a little older or maybe a little rebellious, I would have run from the room and hid under my bed and I think those thoughts even ran through my mind. But this was my mother . . . and all that I had left. So I took that phone and watched her scowling face turn into that honeysuckle smile as I said what she wanted me to say. And as I did it, I could feel something inside me twist like ringing out the wash and I felt like lightning was gonna strike me.

But the sun came up the next day and I was surprised that it didn't bleach away how stained I felt."

"So what happened? Did she marry Carl?"

"Hell, no! That little stunt must have scared the guy to death! We never heard from him again after that! Probably the best thing that could have happened!" Rose exhorted as both she and Melanie burst into laughter. "Maybe next Lenten Season I'll tell you the rest of the story. Or you can wait and read it in my book!"

On the way home from the diner after mid-week Lenten service, Melanie invited Rose to come to Shabbat services at Temple Shalom Lev in two days. Melanie had learned only that day that Rabbi Moishe Robbins was going to be their guest speaker at their Friday Shabbat dinner at the temple prior to services. Melanie was pleased to return the opportunity to have Rose join her to hear Rabbi Robbins, the Spiritual Leader of the largest congregation of Black Jews in the United States, speak.

Rose accepted Melanie's invitation with enthusiasm. Melanie picked Rose up and Trevor stayed home to baby sit with Trev. They arrived at the temple and found their way through the table-lined social hall to a choice table with the best view of the podium. The room filled with congregants wishing one another "Shabbat Shalom" and offering greetings of "Gut Shabbos." Melanie and Rose chatted quietly together until the dinner began with the ceremonial blessings. The candles were lighted and blessed by the president of the Sisterhood, the wine was blessed by the president of the Brotherhood, and Rabbi Levy blessed the challah, the ceremonial braided bread, and dinner was served.

After dinner and the singing of some songs to welcome the Sabbath, the assemblage listened as Rabbi Robbins explained the history of the 65,000 Black Jews in America, known as Falasha Jews, who descended from Solomon and Sheba. Sheba, an Ethiopian, was Black. Rabbi Robbins joked about the burden of being a descendant of a double minority and the double-prejudice felt by Falashas. Nonetheless, his congregants, members of the largest congregation of Black Jews in the U.S., located in Manhattan, were as devoted to Judaism as any other Jew.

Melanie and Rose found Rabbi Robbins' speech fascinating. What was even more fascinating was that the congregation at Shalom Lev made the assumption that Rose, the only Black female present, must be the Rebbitzen of the Falacian Synagogue, the Rabbi's wife. After the services were concluded in the Sanctuary and everyone reassembled in the social hall for the Oneg Shabbat festivities to welcome the Sabbath, Melanie couldn't contain her laughter as she watched members of the congregation surrounding Rose and saying such things as, "You must be very proud of your husband," and asking questions like," What special challenges do you encounter as the Rebbitzen of your synagogue?"

Melanie was delighted to hear Rose respond like an actress who stepped into a role. Instantly, Rose became the Rebbitzen and gave her impromptu answers, enjoying the moment and rolling with the wave of attention. As Rose later explained, "I just spun a yarn! It was great fun!" Melanie and Rose laughed all the way home.

But after Melanie dropped Rose at her home, she was troubled by the nagging sense that she had received the cold shoulder from everybody she approached at the Oneg. As she played the evening back in her mind, she thought something might be brewing that she didn't understand. At first she thought it was everyone's excitement about talking to Rabbi Robbins and to Rose but she still couldn't help but feel she was being left out. As her mind retraced the events of the evening, her thoughts stopped and zoomed in on the moment when she reached the cluster of people that included Dawn. She still couldn't figure out whether she was observing something real and aimed at her or whether she was just imagining that she was getting strange looks from people she knew well, as well as from strangers. It just seemed like Dawn couldn't look Melanie in the eye.

As she pulled into her tree lined driveway, Melanie made a conscious decision not to think about it anymore. People are crazy and I'm not going to make myself crazy trying to sort them out, she thought.

CHAPTER THIRTY-THREE

THE HECTIC PACE of the week, the hours she had spent on The Foundation's projects, the extra time and energy she had put into picking up Allison's piece of the preparation for the Oneg, all left Melanie weary. When she woke up on Saturday morning, every muscle in her body ached. She had pains in the long muscles of her legs and her hips and she was certain that her resistance must be down. She must have caught some viral-something from some coughing-sneezing person and now she would pay for her gregariousness.

As the day progressed, Melanie spent most of it asleep in bed. From time to time she would wake up, drag herself to the kitchen, boil a pot of canned chicken soup, and crawl back to bed with a full mug of steaming liquid. Then she would fall asleep again before the soup was cool enough for her to consume. This was not the path to recovery, Melanie thought.

By sundown, Melanie was starting to feel a little better. Her appetite had returned but she thought that was in exchange for losing her voice. Each time the phone rang, she managed to croak out enough volume to say, "I'm sick and I can't talk," which ended the conversation rapidly.

Melanie, wrapped in her thickest terrycloth robe and shod in her furry pink fuzzy slippers, stood at the stove in her kitchen putting together the fastest, blandest meal she could make herself. As the water came to a rolling boil, she dropped two handfuls of spaghetti into a big pot her mother referred to as," the shissel." Hot spaghetti with a little butter swished over it should do the trick, Melanie thought.

As she stirred the boiling strands, clouds of steam built over the pot and licked around the range hood above the stove, pouring up into Melanie's face. In the steam, as if in a crystal ball, Melanie envisioned the Schwartzes, the Rosenthals, Dawn and her husband and herself standing in front of the moveable wall in the Social Hall. She saw Dawn's face filled with anger, no, rage. She saw the clenched teeth and heard the biting edge to every syllable she delivered in Melanie's direction. "What could she have been thinking?" Melanie wondered. What did I ever do to her? Or anybody else, for that matter?

And then it hit her. From out of the fog of the steaming pot, it hit her like an unexpected storm at sea.

"Oh, my God," Melanie said aloud. Melanie left the boiling pot unattended and ran to her study to find the list of Temple members. There, on the list, was Dawn's name. Melanie frantically dialed her number.

Dawn answered on the first ring. Melanie squeaked out enough volume to say,

"Dawn, it's Melanie. I can barely speak so please listen carefully. Normally, I would wait until I felt a lot better and could speak before I called you but this is too important. And you have to believe how important I thought it was to call you now or calling you would be the last thing on earth I would do. But I'm standing here in a cloud of steam stirring noodles on my stove when it struck me like lightning why you were so strange with me at the Oneg last night. You think I am the one who is supposed to have seen Allison in the lobby of a hotel in New York. You think that, don't you, Dawn?" There was a silence on the other end.

"Dawn, let me tell you directly and as clearly as this crackling voice allows that I never saw Allison anywhere but at the Temple and if I had seen her in a Manhattan hotel lobby I would have thought she was there for the same reason I was: to have a meeting with someone. I have enough lunches and dinners in hotel restaurants not to even consider that the other diners are doing anything more than having a meal and a conversation. If I had seen her, which I didn't, I would never have given it a second thought. So if you're looking for the person who started that story, you need to look elsewhere. It wasn't me. The look on your face last night haunted me until tonight when all of the sudden it hit me like a ton of bricks that you thought I was at the bottom of the rumors and at the root of the troubles between Allison and Dave. You have to believe me that I wouldn't call you directly with a voice and body in this condition if what I am telling you were untrue and I hope you believe me."

"Oh, I never thought you were associated with the rumors," Dawn replied.

It could only be contributed to Melanie's physically weakened state that the words she was thinking came out of her mouth. "Well, now one of us is not being completely honest," Melanie replied. "It was painted all over you, Dawn, but I didn't put it together until tonight. I heard some women in the coatroom gossiping about the sad situation between Allison and Dave and it all fell together not five minutes ago in my mind."

"Thank you for calling, Melanie. I do believe you and appreciate your call. Feel better. Good night."

Melanie stood there with the telephone receiver in her hand, wondering if the rumor that was pinned on her would be removed, or would she carry the telltale stigma of being wrapped in a web not of her doing?

The best way to fix this is to call Allison, Melanie thought. When she reached only the answer machine at the Shapiro residence, Melanie left a simple message with her name and telephone number and the instructions: Call me.

Two days later, Allison called. Melanie was feeling much better and able to speak without pain on her part and suffering for the listener. Melanie told Allison of her experience at the Temple, the strange responses of people to her, the steely-cold attitude of Dawn, the conversation in the coatroom, and of her call to Dawn.

"I can only guess that somebody started telling people that you went to the city and were there with someone and decided that, because I go into the city for meetings and stay over from time to time, that I must have been the one who saw you. I just want you to know, Allison, that it wasn't me," Melanie testified.

"I know it wasn't you, Mel. I think I've got a real good idea of exactly who it was. I've only been to the city one time, Mel. And the only thing dirty that happened was that a tablecloth got soiled in a restaurant. Besides, the day that happened was the day you went into the hospital for your yearly physical. So I know it wasn't you, Mel. And I'm so sorry you got dragged into this story for no reason."

"I'm so glad you understand and believe me, Allison. That's why I called Dawn and you because you were the only two people that mattered. I really don't care one bit what the gossip mongers think! But I do care what you think. I'm so glad you got my message and called me back."

"Message? I didn't get a message, Mel. I called because I wanted to speak to you. Where did you leave me a message?"

"On your answer machine at home."

"Home has a whole new meaning, Mel. I moved out. With the kids. I'm living in the Summer building of The Seasons complex."

"Hoo-haa! Fancy-shmancy!" Melanie chided.

""Stop that," Allison said, laughing. "I'm in too much pain to laugh. But you're right. This place is just fabulous. Elegant. Marvelous . . ."

"Enough, already. I get the point."

"I hope when the dust settles you'll come over and visit. Let me give you my new land line and cell phone numbers."

"How did you get in there and get a phone so fast?" Melanie quizzed her, with great appreciation of the accomplishment.

"That's another long story for another day," Allison replied, giving her the vital statistics regarding address and telephone contact information.

They said goodbye. Melanie felt so much better, like a huge weight had been lifted from her shoulders. How horrible people could be, in so many ways, on so many levels. So much deceit. So many rumors and so many lies.

CHAPTER THIRTY-FOUR

WHILE THE RUMOR about Allison's supposed tryst in the city attached itself to Melanie with relative ease, disconnecting Melanie as the source and cause of the breakup of the perfect couple was not as easy. Not everyone who heard the original version got the revised edition. As a matter of fact, the truth did not have the same momentum as the lie.

Dawn saw no reason to retell anything to anyone. She was too busy propping up baby brother and his not so empty life. Sylvie moved back into the house. After all, Dave needed someone to clean his house and cook his dinner on the nights that Dawn couldn't be available to perform that function. And eating alone in restaurants got pretty boring and exaggerated Dave's already great sense of loss.

On the other hand, Dave saw no reason why he should have to clean up after himself and offered Sylvie the opportunity to resume her job, and move back in as au pair to himself. Sylvie was doing a great job filling the empty spaces. She brought the lightheartedness of a barely out of her teens young woman with a European flair and French charm. She made sure that the house was immaculate, a not so difficult task considering that there were no children to mess the place up, one adult who was out of the house all day, and only one bed to make in the morning. Sylvie did a great job at everything she touched in every room, including the bedroom. While Dave was pitied and babied and given support by all concerned, Sylvie made sure his every need was met. And Allison was referred to only on rare occasions so as not to upset the family, and when she was mentioned it was only by her new name, The Bitch.

Melanie suffered too. Backs continued to turn as she approached. People she hardly knew turned away from her. Everyone's reaction to something she had absolutely nothing to do with gave her new insights into why she generally kept her distance from people. They were just not to be trusted. Again, she remembered Clair Booth Luce's famous quote: "No good deed will go unpunished" and the motto of her piano teacher:" The more people I meet, the more I like my dog." Look what she found herself embroiled in just by putting herself in proximity to Allison.

"Maybe I shouldn't volunteer to do anything again. Now that's a thought," Melanie mused.

The whole episode made it incredibly easy for Melanie to decide to pack up and move to the city. There was nothing here for her anyway. She was surrounded by couples and everybody else's family. With the addition of being the community outcast and scapegoat for the breakup of Allison and Dave Shapiro, Melanie had come to the end of the line.

They're all nuts here, Melanie mused. *What am I doing here surrounded by people running in gigantic circles trying to prove to one another that they are the best and have the best while not caring one bit about who they step on or over in their search for the perfect mask to their private inadequacies.*

I'm out of here, Melanie thought decisively.

There was enormous joy and enormous power in her decision. There was excitement and drama. She was on the way to a bright, new episode in her life that dazzled her imagination.

In fact, it was David King who dazzled her.

Melanie set about preparing for the big move. She made lists of things that had to be done. Her lists had lists. They ranged from the primary list of the major tasks to be attended to and the secondary lists that corresponded to all of the big areas.

She decided not to sell the house but to leave it and its contents in place. But she'd need a bigger place in New York. With a view. A wrap-around view.

Windows everywhere. And high up like her studio so she could see at least one of the rivers that envelop Manhattan island.

Call realtors in NYC. Find Apt. Buy Furniture. (Go to Bloomingdale's for ideas). Pack clothes. Buy dishes and kitchen utensils. Get mover to transfer clothes and knick-knacks. Take the Jieng painting to NYC. Take the Tarkays to NYC (make sure mover wraps them well) . . .

The list went on and on and grew daily with items that needed attention. Included among them was her promise to Rose to go to a Wednesday night Lenten Service at her church. Melanie decided she would make the trip back to Long Island to spend that evening with Rose. After calling Rose to confirm that date, Melanie attended to the last item on the list which was the most important one to her: Say goodbye to Rabbi Levy.

*   *   *

Melanie dropped into the temple the day before the movers were to come to finalize her exit from the town where she had spent so much of her life. The apartment was ready and waiting for the last of her personal effects to arrive from Long Island and from her NYC studio. Everything was exactly as she planned it to be, down to the last brass doorknob and porcelain switch plate cover. The apartment was right out of Metropolitan Home and Melanie considered herself lucky to have found it and grabbed it. The rent was ridiculous but, after all, this was New York.

Melanie entered the rabbi's study. He was seated behind mountains of paper on his desk.

"Please, Melanie, sit down."

"Thank you for taking the time to see me, Rabbi. I see you have a lot of work in front of you."

"It's incredible. And I'm leaving in two weeks for Israel. I don't know how I'm going to get it all done."

"I make lists, Rabbi. Then I just munch away at the items, one line at a time. It makes me feel good every time I get to cross off the list something that I've accomplished. Of course, the list keeps getting longer on the bottom so I never really get done."

"So the answer, then, is 'Just do it!'"

"That's it, Rabbi."

The rabbi smiled his impish smile and in a quiet voice and change of focus from himself to Melanie said, "So, tell me what brings you to me today."

"I'm closing up the house for a while, Rabbi. I'm moving into the city. I've got an apartment all ready and tomorrow the last of my belongings that I want to take with me will move. I've given up my NYC studio and consolidating my prized possessions into the new apartment. I'm excited about it and I think it will offer me a whole new world of opportunity. But I realized something during the whole process."

"What's that, Melanie?"

"It wasn't so hard to find a new occupation. And it wasn't so hard to find a new place to live. But I don't think it's not going to be easy to find a new rabbi. Not one like you."

"Melanie, I will always be your rabbi. You remember that wherever you go."

Tears welled in Melanie's eyes. That was no surprise to her. What did surprise her was that there were tears in her rabbi's eyes, too.

"Thank you, Rabbi. I will keep in touch. I promise.

"I'm really glad that you've picked tomorrow to move, Mel."

"Why is that?"

"Because tomorrow is Tuesday."

"So?"

"So, according to the Torah, God created the universe in six days and rested on the seventh. For us, the seventh day, Shabbat, is Saturday. So if you count backwards, God started creation on a Sunday. If you look at Genesis, you'll see that every day, God looked carefully at what had been created and declared that," It was good." That was true for Sunday's work and Monday's work. But on Tuesday, God said," It was good," twice, not once. So Tuesday is a special day that is filled with twice as much 'goodness.' If you're going to do something that has important meaning in your life, Tuesday is a very good day to do it!"

The rabbi beamed, letting Melanie know that somewhere in her plans and the rabbi's story, there was a special blessing for her.

"Always the teacher, rabbi," Melanie said, smiling at the rabbi through welling tears. "I'll miss you."

Melanie left Temple Shalom Lev knowing this was the last time she would walk through these doors as a congregant, knowing that in years to come, if she visited, she would come back as a stranger to the new crop of members putting their children through the Hebrew School. And knowing that there was nothing and no one there she would miss except her rabbi. Her rabbi. Even he had confirmed that fact.

On Tuesday morning, at 7:45am, a large truck with three huge men, armed with putrid smelling quilted canvas blankets, descended into her rain-drenched driveway, splashing through every available puddle on their way to her front door. This was not the blessed Tuesday Melanie expected.

"How long is it going to take you to pack me up and get me out of here?" Melanie asked.

"It's going to take most of the day, Ma'am. This artwork and some of the other pieces have to be carefully wrapped."

Good grief, Melanie thought. Imagine if I were moving everything!

The day could be best described as English weather. It was gray, misty, rainy and all together sloppy outside with the accompanying damp chill air. Melanie's day was filled with gray moments of nostalgia as the men carried memories of her life in that house out to the truck.

The day wore on. When Melanie glanced at the clock on the oven, she couldn't believe it was already 3:00PM. Melanie had always thought of that hour as liberating: school's over for the day. Funny, how childhood routines stay with you all through your life.

Looking on the bright side, Melanie was glad that, since it was so late in the day, she would have a chance to run by and give Rose and Trev a hug before she moved into the city.

Melanie was right about the events that 3:00pm bring. Trev and his best friend, Randy, were at that very moment, bounding out of the front door of the school yelling their goodbyes to their friends as they passed. The two boys jabbered away until they reached the curb where the school buses were lined up.

"Well, okay, Trev. I'll see ya tomorrow," Randy said as he skipped off in the direction of his bus. Trev made his way through the crowd of children, weaving a path to bus number 7. Trev was bursting inside with a plan he had been brewing all day ever since Randy's mom appeared at school with cupcakes to celebrate Randy's birthday. Trev had been hatching a plan to surprise him after school with a present, something Randy had wanted and admired every time they played together.

The bus ride home didn't go fast enough for Trevor. When the bus finally reached Trevor's stop, he leaped off in one grand move into Rose's waiting arms.

"Come on, Mom! We've gotta move!"

"Wait a minute, son. What's your hurry?"

"Come on! I've got a plan!"

"You do, now," Rose responded, quizzically.

"Yeah, so come on," Trev shouted over his shoulder as he ran ahead to his house.

Trevor swung the storm door open wide. It slammed behind him as he raced up the stairs to his room. Rose entered the foyer and yelled upstairs to Trev, "What on earth are you up to, young man?"

At that moment, Trev emerged from his room and raced downstairs with a little package wrapped in colorful paper and a ribbon he had saved from a Christmas present.

"What's that, Trev?"

"It's my amethyst crystal I got at the museum. Randy likes it a lot. When I brought it to school for 'Show and Tell,' we played Space Station with it. He thought it was cool. I want to give it to him. Today's his birthday. His mom brought cupcakes to school today. That's how I know! Please drive me to his house, mom so I can give it to him. I've been planning this all day." Trevor delivered his explanation in one breath.

"I don't know where Randy lives," Rose answered with a worried look on her face.

"That's okay, mom, because I do!" Trev responded, proudly.

"Why don't you just give it to him tomorrow?" Rose asked, tenderly. "Or you could give it to him Sunday when you see him at church. I'm sure he'll have a Sunday School celebration of his birthday, too."

"But today is his REAL BIRTHDAY, mom," Trev replied, trying to stress the difference. "And I want him to have it today. PLEASE take me. There are big streets to cross if I go on my bike."

"Well, at least you've got that part right. Don't try going over there yourself, young man. There are too many busy roads to cross."

"Wait a minute. I thought you didn't know where Randy lives," Trev snapped back with a Sherlock Holmes air of discovery.

"Well, I know, more or less, where they live but not the exact location," Rose said, trying to set the record straight for the little detective.

Trev didn't understand Rose's reluctance. He wasn't asking anything impossible. Today was a free day: no soccer practice, no Little League, no company. But there was homework to be done.

"Come on, Ma," he urged. "I want to get there before he goes to the library or something."

"All right, son. But we've got to come right back. You have homework to do. Be sure to take the address."

"Don't worry," he beamed at her. "I've got the address memorized. I just want to give him his present now and then we can come right back. I have a spelling test to study for but I'll get that done. I'm good at spelling," he smiled, proudly.

The car couldn't move fast enough for Trev. He urged Rose to drive faster. She used the opportunity to give Trev a lesson in safe driving practices . . . regardless of the reason for the hurry. They twisted and turned through the back roads and lanes of the beautiful tree-lined streets, finally arriving at Randy's house. Rose found a spot to park in front of the neighboring house.

"Go ahead, Trev. I'll wait here."

"Okay, Mom. I'll be right back. Don't look so worried. I'll get my homework done!"

The sound of the slamming car door could not cover the noise of Trev's pounding heart. All he could think of was how happy Randy would be when he saw that crystal. Now he could play "Space Station" all the time and pretend that the crystal provided all the energy and magical ingredients for Pretend Space Travel.

Trev raced up the steps two at a time. A bunch of balloons was tied to the railing next to the front door to welcome Randy home on his birthday. Trev rang the doorbell. He could hear the television on loudly through the door. There was no answer.

He rang again and, in quick succession, knocked loudly. "Gee, they've got that TV on loud," he thought.

Then the door opened. The TV sounded even louder now. A tall blond lady simply said," Yes?"

Trevor recognized her as Randy's mom, Mrs. Corbet, one of the Sunday School teachers at Church.

"Hi, I'm Trevor Winston. I want to give this to Randy for his . . ."

Randy appeared at the door behind the tall lady. Trev noticed that he wasn't wearing the clothes he wore to school . . . and he wasn't wearing after-school play clothes.

"Hey, Mom, this is Trevor, my friend from school. Hey, Trev," Randy smiled.

"I brought you this, Randy. For your birthday."

Suddenly, Trevor realized that the loud voices were not from the television. Children wearing party hats pressed behind Randy and his mother yelling friendly greetings to Trevor. Trevor knew everyone there.

"Hi," is all that Trevor could say. "I wanted you to have this, Randy." Trevor held out the little brightly wrapped package.

"Gee, thanks, Trev. I can't wait to open it."

"Thank you for coming by Trevor. Randolph will see you at school tomorrow."

The door closed.

Trevor stood there, frozen in place for a moment, staring at the big white door.

Suddenly, as if lightning had struck the ground next to him, Trevor took off, running faster than his feet had ever moved at any Little League game, racing back to the safety of the car, back to his mother who sat behind the wheel of the car with tears streaming down her face.

Trevor stood on the grass outside the car and looked at his mother through the window.

Trevor knew his mother expected exactly what happened.

Trevor said nothing.

Rose said, "Get in the car, Trevor. We have a spelling test to study for."

The drive home took forever. Trevor replayed the afternoon in his mind. What just happened?

Trev was quiet all the way home. Rose suffered the quiet pain that comes with motherhood. She searched her mind for the right opening phrase passing on such thoughts as, "How are you doin', baby," or "Are you okay?" or "Do you want to talk about it?" Finally, Rose said, "I feel so bad for Randy. His mama has done him a great disservice."

Trevor looked at Rose and said, "You're right, mama. Randy and I are great friends. I know he didn't forget about me. He couldn't have."

"I know, darlin'. I know."

They arrived at their house. Rose drove into the garage and Trevor jumped out of the car, racing up to his room to start his homework. Rose made herself a cup of tea and sat down at the kitchen table. Tears streamed uncontrollably down her face. How could that woman call herself a church member, a Sunday School teacher, Dear Lord, what a hypocrite!

Rose's thoughts were interrupted by the phone ringing. Rose dried her eyes, blew her nose, and reached for the phone. The sound of her voice clearly indicated that she had been crying.

"Hey, there. I just called to say I'm all packed up and to see if you were there for me to drop by on my way out of town but you don't sound so good. What's the matter, Rose? Are you all right?" Melanie asked.

"No, I'm not," Rose declared, as she began to cry again.

"What's the matter?"

"Well," she muttered, "the matter is I thought I prepared my son for the devils in the world but I forgot to prepare him for the devils in the church."

Melanie said she'd be right over and raced to Rose's home. Rose told Melanie the whole story. And when she reached the part about the fair-haired kids on the other side of the doorway, adorned with party hats and enveloped by balloons, a doorway that was guarded by a tall blond dragon, Melanie and Rose sobbed together. This was an awful way to spend their last afternoon together. Was there any hope for the world?

CHAPTER THIRTY-FIVE

D AVID KING WAS a visionary. If he had a fault, it was that he was usually twenty years ahead of his time, making it difficult for his ideas to be easily accepted by those less forward-thinking. He was a framer, not a detail man. And he was a talker, not a listener.

But from the first moment, it was clear that Melanie understood where he wanted to go and knew exactly how to get him there. It took some time for David to give Melanie an assignment without outlining every single detail of what needed to be done to complete the job.

"I know what you want, David," Melanie protested. "Let me just go and do it and if you don't like it, we'll trash it. But please let me out of here so I can get started before the day is over. You're just wasting time going over every little thing."

After several repeat performances of that little scene, which always ended with David exclaiming that Melanie completed the task beyond his expectations and better than he would have done had he done it himself, he finally gave Melanie the latitude she needed to do whatever had to be done. She had, in fact, grown into the description he had outlined at the diner: someone who could be his right arm, right and left leg, and half of his brain.

They became, in short, an unbeatable team. Together, they encompassed every skill a company needed to be successful. All they had to do to round out the picture was to put worker bees in place to carryout their master plan. In the business world, even that wasn't easy.

"My father and my grandfather used to complain about the same problem," Melanie lamented. "My grandfather used to say, 'The trouble today is you just can't get good help!' And I was just four years old at the time! Nothing has changed."

"You're right," David replied. "But with you at my side, I have no fear. I know that, if we had nobody else, if we had to let everybody go tomorrow, between the two of us we have all of the skills in every area to get the job done."

The next twelve months were filled with excitement and long hours as David and Melanie worked long, hard, and smart, focused on the growth of the company. David was consumed with his goal which, after six months, he shared with Melanie. She wasn't entirely surprised by David's news that he wanted to take the company public. It was the trendy thing to do and the place where big dreams became bankable realities.

While David spent never less than sixty hours each week at the office and often traveled for days, sometimes weeks, at a time, chasing opportunities for the company, Allison was left to her own resources. She saw David only at his convenience. And while he talked about how much he cared about her, he was both emotionally and physically unavailable, leaving the black hole she felt inside gnawing at her.

As Melanie's life took on new meaning, added new facets, became more exciting, Allison's life diminished proportionately. As David became a more important part of Melanie's life and routine, Allison saw less and less of David.

Dave made a weekly deposit to Allison's checking account for child support. Every other weekend Dave would come and pick the children up on Friday and deliver them home on Sunday at 6:00pm. He made a point of dropping Sylvie off at the shopping arcade in the Winter Building of the Four Seasons complex and then picking her back up after he had the children in tow to avoid any confrontation on the subject.

With the rent paid by David and child support paid by Dave, that still left Allison with things to worry about. She found a part time job teaching in a local nursery school so she was able to take both children with her and avoid childcare costs which would have wiped out any earnings she might otherwise have made. But after taxes and gasoline and other incidental expenses, Allison did not have much left over. It was clear that next year she would need to have a fulltime good paying job since the twelve month prepayment of rent was well on its way to coming to an end and she and David were no closer than they were when she moved out of her home and into this new life. His immersion in his business' growth left them with precious little time for each other.

It wasn't that Allison didn't want to bring the subject up of their future together; it was more that there never was an opportunity to really spend time with him. When he called, the subject of the conversation was always the same: him. He would talk animatedly about a new challenge, a new deal, a new meeting, a new opportunity, a new conquest, and a bright new tomorrow which focused entirely on business. After a perfunctory, "How are you and the kids," the monologue on The Life and Times of David King began and would end abruptly when another call or interruption presented itself, prompting the concluding words: "Gotta go."

Allison wasn't really sure how she arrived at this place in her life and where everything went wrong. But one thing was clear. There was no going back. Here was where she was and here was where she had to lay her stakes to build her own exhilarating future, whatever that meant. But failure was not an option because it wasn't just her life at stake. Jennifer and Joshua were sitting in the wings and their future depended on her performance. If for no other reason, Allison was determined to make everything work.

So was Sylvie. She was determined to make everything work for her. And the only way to do that was to keep Dave happy. To do that, she reasoned, she had to get Dave's kids back for him and for her. That would make them a family. That would give the children the loving daddy and mommy they deserved. All she had to do was figure out a way to remove Allison from the picture.

While Sylvie schemed and plotted at her end, playing the perfect 'wife' to Dave as they "played house," Allison sent out resumes and responded to classified ads. She was convinced that she had to position herself financially before the twelve months were up or she would be in big trouble. Except as an act of charity, there would be no reason for David King to continue this arrangement. Allison was an inconvenience in his life, a luxury for which he had no time.

When she was called back for a second interview for a teaching position in a local school district, Allison was thrilled. Now having passed muster with the assistant principal and the principal, Allison was offered a position teaching third grade commencing in September. Between her salary and child support and the few months still left prepaid on her apartment, Allison felt she would be in good shape. If need be, she would look for a less expensive place to live, but, for the moment, that would wait.

The school secretary gave Allison a packet of forms that needed to be filled out: IRS forms, pension plan forms, parking space forms, teachers' union forms, and medical forms that were all required to be appropriately filed before August 1. While the teaching staff was off for the summer, the secretaries and janitors only got two weeks vacation, the secretary explained with the tone that communicated a message somewhere between the fact that they were indispensable and that they were getting screwed.

Allison smiled and scooped up all of the papers. She was ecstatic. She had set a goal and achieved it. Nothing was as sweet as the taste of success and achievement. She was going to be on her own, independent, self-sustaining, answering to no one and the best third grade teacher that school had ever seen.

Before her nanny was even out the door, Allison had the school forms spread out on the kitchen table and, with one hand, reached for the telephone to make the appointment with her physician to fill out the one form she could not complete on her own. The sooner I get all of this paperwork done, the sooner my mind will be at ease, Allison thought.

As she lifted the receiver, she was surprised that there was no dial tone. She tapped the buttons on the telephone several times hoping the dial tone would appear. Thinking she heard something on the other end, Allison said, "Hello? Is anybody there?"

"Allison, is that you?"

"Yes. Who is this?

"It's me. David. What's going on?"

"David!" she responded with delight. "I had just . . ."

"It's who? What does he want? All right, all right. Tell him I'll talk to him. Allison, you gonna be home? I'll call you right back." The conversation came to an abrupt conclusion even before it could begin, without David waiting for a reply of any kind.

"I had just picked up the phone to make a call and there you were . . . no dial tone or ringing phone or anything," Allison said, completing her thought for the benefit of no one but herself. "Sure, David, call me when you get around to it," she mumbled to herself.

While David's interruption did not change the course of Allison's plan, it did deflate her enthusiasm. His almost-call definitely rained on her parade. But it didn't stop the momentum of her conviction to her course. Once again, Allison picked up the telephone, reached her doctor's office, made her appointment for a physical for the Board of Education, and left the receiver off the hook at the end of the call. She didn't want to be available when David called back. She had had so little of David that it was beginning to be quite enough.

CHAPTER THIRTY-SIX

D AVID FOLLOWED EVERY path carefully that he had outlined in his plan to expand his company and take it public. He met with investment bankers. He met with underwriters. He met with private investors with public shells. And at every meeting, he had Melanie at his side to help him evaluate each and every opportunity, to catch the things he missed, to ask the questions he didn't ask, and to observe every detail that he didn't focus on as he assessed the "big picture." And after every meeting, he would ask Melanie the same question: "So what did you learn?"

The first time David did that, Melanie panicked at the question. Being put on the spot by the president of the company was like being asked to stand on quicksand. What if she had the wrong answer? What if she didn't learn what he wanted her to learn? What if she didn't learn anything? What if he thought she was an idiot? This was not an easy spot to be in.

But after the surprise of the first time, Melanie expected the inevitable question. Her intellect, her knowledge, and her intuition were resources that David had come to rely on. Melanie grew to be comfortable expressing her ideas and opinions to David. He had complete confidence in her and repeatedly reminded her of how lucky he was to have her on his team. They were invincible.

In the course of exploring the world of capitalization, David hit on a company that promised to deliver everything necessary to take his company public. They inflamed his spirit and his imagination.

They came to David through an ad he had placed in the Wall Street Journal. Unlike all the previous explorations, the principals wanted to meet with David only. Melanie was clearly excluded. She referred to them as Macho Pigs, Inc.

After several visits to their offices, they were scheduled to come to David's office. The appointment was made for 4:45pm. When they arrived, they were ushered into David's office and the door was closed by one of the visitors.

At 5:00pm, the entire staff left in their usual mass movement. Only Melanie remained behind. Melanie, the confidant. Melanie, the right arm, left leg, right leg, and half of David's brain. Melanie, the excluded.

The temperature in the office got higher and the air quality stuffier as the building shut down the ventilation system for the day. Melanie went to David's door and opened it, saying," Everyone's gone for the day. It's getting stuffy in here. I thought you might want to leave the door open."

Had it been David's choice, the door would have been open and Melanie would have been in the room. But the choice was on the side of the money.

"That's all right. You can close it," was the remark from one of the three visitors.

The temperature in the office could not compare to Melanie's personal rising thermostat.

Two hours later, when the visitors left, David brought Melanie up-to-date on everything that was going on. There were no secrets between them.

David tried to call Allison to share the news that he had hit on a company that wanted to put millions of dollars into his company as a first step to taking it public. David would maintain controlling interest and have all of the funds necessary to grow the company to new heights. He would have liked to have shared the joyful news with Allison but he couldn't get through the busy signal on her land line and her cell phone went straight to voice mail. So he gave up. He was tired and had enough for the day. Time to call it a day. He and Melanie walked to the elevator and recapped what they had to do tomorrow. Melanie recapped how she hated these rude people with the manners of barnyard animals.

While David yawned and stretched to give himself the power and energy to get home, Allison crawled off to bed, having tucked the children in for the night. She was exhausted. Even with the daytime help of a nanny and a maid, taking care of the apartment, the two toddlers, running around doing chores, and getting up in the middle of the night to comfort Josh and Jen who still were adjusting to not living with Daddy, was all taking its toll on Allison and she knew it. She worried that taking on a full time teaching job might sap her of what energy she had left but she decided that she would take up a hobby to relax: being a couch potato. She was going to give herself permission to be idle and do nothing of socially redeeming value. She was going to take every unplanned moment and lie down like lox on a platter. She would actively drive any thoughts from her mind that prompted her to get up and do something. The moves, the adjustments, the children, the two Davids, were all getting to her. Everything could wait.

Allison climbed into bed under the fluffy down comforter and burrowed her head into three soft pillows neatly arranged so that her head could not roll off an edge. She hoped she would make it until morning before she was awakened. She drove out the simple facts that made no sense: a restaurant meeting which led to nothing, created a bedroom fantasy that led to the break-up of a marriage. How did that happen?

As Allison was climbing into bed mulling these thought, Sylvie was turning back the covers on the bed she shared with Dave. Hotel style, she bent back the left and right side of the bed linens so that they resembled turned down pages of a book. All that was missing was the sweet treat on the pillowcases. Sylvie planned to replace that amenity.

By the time Dave came out of the shower, Sylvie was clad in a little sheer black number from the Victoria's Secret catalog. It was worth its weight in hormones. Dave responded instantly to his little French pastry. It was incredible how he was seen as the victim and Allison was The Bitch.

Sylvie finished her nightly performance with her nightly prayers which were said in the same fashion in which she had been saying them since childhood, kneeling at the side of the bed, hands clasped in front of her, eyes closed. And the prayers always ended the same way, and for Dave's benefit:" . . . and may Dave's family be reunited with him in love and peace. Amen."

CHAPTER THIRTY-SEVEN

IT WAS TUESDAY. Allison had showered and prepared to go to her doctor's office. She would have the nurse fill out all the forms in all the right places. Then she would drop off the whole packet of papers to the school secretary months in advance of their due date. That had to be a sign that she was on track and making progress.

The doctor took all of the routine tests. Blood, urine, blood pressure. Then there was the battery of x-rays and smears. When all the prodding, poking, and probing came to an end, she dressed and left the examining room. Allison was asked to wait in the reception area. This medical group was particularly advanced and did all their own lab work on the premises. In a few minutes, she would be seen by the doctor who could give her the forms and that would be that for another year.

Allison waited and waited. No one ever seemed to rush in a doctor's office. Finally, her name was called and she entered the doctor's private office. Again she waited and waited until he finally arrived, clipboard in hand.

"Hello, Allison. It's been a while," the doctor began.

"Yes, Doctor. I've just been so busy."

"It's never good to neglect yourself, Allison, no matter how busy you get."

"You're right. I know that. But time just flies." Allison couldn't believe she said anything that dumb. But the doctor's mundane banter was getting on her nerves. What she wanted to say was, "Give me my papers already and let me out of here," but that would not be a good idea. This was the doctor's turf and she had to respect his kingdom.

"Allison, I'm quite concerned about you. We checked and rechecked your test and x-rays three times to be sure there was no mistake. I called in two other physicians on our team. And there is no mistake . . ."

Allison didn't hear one word the doctor said after that point. The look on his face made it clear that this was not going to be a pretty story. As the temporary cloud lifted from her fogged brain, Allison heard only one phrase: inoperable lymphoma . . . six weeks . . .

Allison's thoughts were with two people only. Not the two Davids but with her children. The pain was beyond description. They would be cheated out of the mother who adored them. She would not be there for all the special little joys, the benchmark achievements, the painful experiences. What could be more painful for them than losing their mother.

The worst of it was there was no place for them to go but to Dave. And Sylvie. What cruel punishment was this?

Allison went home in a daze. She hugged the children and ask Nanny to pack their toys and clothes. They were going to visit Daddy for a while and they'd all be taking a ride there tonight.

Mommy's tiredness was more than just fatigue and Mommy needed special rest. Maybe a very long rest. It would be a good idea if they got all settled in back at their house so everybody was comfortable while Mommy rested.

Allison wondered how she would tell David. Or if he'd even notice she was gone.

We won't have to worry about what happens when the twelve months of payments runs out, she thought in a moment of bizarre irony.

I don't think anyone will notice I'm gone.

Allison summoned the courage to call Dave and tell him about the reunion with his children he was about to have.

CHAPTER THIRTY-EIGHT

IT WAS TUESDAY. Dave showered with Sylvie and prepared to meet the day. Not a bad life.

Sylvie made the one bed that needed making and straightened the bathroom while Dave dressed. She ran downstairs and started breakfast, pouring orange juice into the glasses that were set at the table when dinner was cleared away.

Sylvie was going to the supermarket today. Dave would drop her on his way to work and she would take a taxi back to the house. One day, Sylvie hoped, she, too, would have a car.

When Dave got to work, he hung up his jacket and sat down at his desk the way he had more than a thousand times before. He had no idea how much his sense of control would change today. He really believed he had it all together.

Dave settled into his routine. In mid-afternoon, he was surprised to learn that Allison was on the phone for him. She never called except on the Fridays when he was supposed to pick up the kids. Dave checked the calendar to be sure he had the date right. It was only Tuesday.

"What is it, Allison?"

"Dave, I don't know how to say this except to say it," Allison said, her voice shaking.

"What now?" Dave asked, unsympathetically.

"I've packed the kids up and I'm bringing them back to live with you," Allison continued slowly and methodically, as though to keep moving before she stopped permanently.

"Now that's a switch. It's enough you don't want your husband. Now you don't want your kids either?"

"I have no more time left in my life to go places that do me no good," Allison responded with greater meaning than Dave could comprehend. "So, I'm not going to deal with your remark at all. As a matter of fact, I'm not going to dignify you or your remarks with any explanation at all. I'm going to drop the kids off with you and then I'm going to the airport and head south. I'm going to go visit my folks in Florida for a while."

"How long will you be there?"

"I'm planning on staying there about six weeks. I know that you and Sylvie will take good care of the kids in my absence. Sylvie has always treated them like her own, anyway. I'm sure it will be good for them to be in familiar surroundings and spend more time with their Dad. God knows they've had plenty of Mom so I think this will be good for them for a change."

"You're lucky to be able to just pick up when you want, dump the kids here and go," Dave snapped back bitterly.

"Yeah, Dave. Real lucky," Allison managed to say, holding back tears just thinking about leaving her children at what was now Dave and Sylvie's house, turning away, getting in her car and driving away from them knowing that would be the last time they would ever see one another in this lifetime. "Real lucky," she repeated. "Listen, I've got to go now. I'm coming out this evening because I'm going to catch an early flight tomorrow and I want to get them all settled so they'll wake up in their own beds out there and start the day off right. I'll try to get them there just after you get home. We'll stop and get Mc Donald's along the way so you won't have to deal with them for dinner tonight."

"Okay. That'll work," Dave said weakly. While he loved his kids and looked forward to their visit, it sure would put an end to those morning showers with Sylvie.

"I don't want to give you too many instructions, Dave, but I do want to tell you one thing. Do your very best for them every day that I am gone so I will have peace of mind where they are concerned. Can I count on that from you, Dave?"

There was something strange and compelling in Allison's voice that Dave didn't know how to respond to but he could certainly relate to the content. While he wanted to just say, "Yes," the bitterness in him over the course of events in their family overrode his better instincts and he responded with a curt," If you're so damned worried about them, why don't you stay home and take care of them yourself?"

"Was that a yes?" Allison asked, elevated to a new plane that did not allow her to get sucked into the trap Dave had set to start a new argument.

"Sure, it's a yes."

"That's all I wanted to hear," Allison replied. "I have to get ready to leave now. I have a lot to do and very little time to do it in," Allison said with resignation and profound meaning far beyond the superficial words and far beyond Dave's grasp.

CHAPTER THIRTY-NINE

I T WAS TUESDAY. David showered and got ready to give God His Glory, Glory. He was exuberant. Manic. This was going to be a day to remember. The men were coming in to finalize the infusion of money into David's company. David was ecstatic. Melanie was skeptical. There was just something about them she didn't like. David insisted it was their excluding her that bothered Melanie and nothing more. Melanie was troubled about their secretive approach to everything including saying "hello."

David had encouraged Melanie to discredit them if she could. He didn't want to get into a relationship with the "wrong people" either. If they were phonies, or frauds, or thieves, or people with questionable reputations, this is not what he wanted. He had a squeaky clean company that he worked hard and long to build.

So he set Melanie loose with all of her resourcefulness to find him a reason why he should not do business with these people.

Melanie tried her damnedest. She left no rock unturned. Nothing turned up. They checked out financially. She used detectives. Everyone checked out okay. She contacted an old college friend who married a NARC. Amazing what you can learn with something as simple as a social security number and a friend in the right places. Unfortunately, Melanie did not find the dirt she was looking for. As a matter of fact, the gentlemen all checked out as squeaky clean as David's company. The report that came back was, "Clean as a whistle. Not even a parking ticket."

That, alone, frightened Melanie. Maybe they were all dirty but with friends in high places so they checked out clean. Or maybe they were hired as a front because they are clean but the money behind them is dirty.

David laughed at Melanie's apprehensions. He was a bottom line man. And the bottom line was that they checked out clean and they had the money. There was no more to talk about. They were coming over today to finalize the deal and by tomorrow the money would be cleared funds in the bank. Glory be to Tuesday.

The staff was given the word to "police the area. Clean up your desk and around.

Look sharp. The money is coming. The money is coming."

Yes, it was a day filled with excitement and jubilation, Melanie thought. After all, if she couldn't find anything on these people, there just must be nothing to find except a bunch of macho pig rude creatures. So, get happy and get on the success bandwagon, she told herself.

At 1:00pm, the men arrived. David's office door was closed. The papers were signed, sealed and delivered. The check was photocopied for the file, and the CFO ran like a bandit to the bank to get it deposited before the close of the business day.

"Hallelujah, we're in the money," David said to Melanie after the men left, without acknowledging her at all. He grabbed Melanie's hands and twirled her around like they were performing a step in a square dance. The two laughed and jumped in the air like cartoon characters, once for each zero following the first numeral on the check."

"That is a sight to behold, darlin'," David exploded.

"We should make a deposit like that at least once a week!" Melanie replied.

"Ain't that the truth," David answered, pulling her into his arms to share his joy.

"Life is good, my dear. Life is good," David concluded." And by the way, let our CFO know that they are sending over their accountant at 4:00pm tomorrow to review our current budget since the papers we gave them reflect the last quarter. They want to have a benchmark from today so they can see where we go with their money to calculate their return on investment."

"She's at the bank, David. She wanted the privilege of depositing the check herself. But I'll tell her when she gets back," Melanie promised.

When David couldn't reach Allison on the first try, he asked Melanie to join him for a celebration drink. At 7:30pm, they left the building and went to a little French bistro on the upper east side of the city to sip one of the hundreds of champagnes the cafe was known for. They toasted with every sip until they had finished the bottle. No champagne was as bubbly as they were.

The only thing higher than they were was the plane carrying Allison to Florida where she would play out the last act of her life in the care of her parents. Neither Dave nor David would see her alive again.

CHAPTER FORTY

WHILE NEITHER MELANIE nor David could forget about the events of the previous afternoon, Wednesday seemed like any other day. The phones rang incessantly, as always. There was the predictable crisis of the day to deal with. Appointments came and went. Life went on. David tried to get Allison but was unsuccessful on the first try and didn't try again. Everyone in the company was busy and stretched to their limits of efficiency. Things were normal.

The day passed quickly. At 2:00pm the CFO informed Melanie and David that the check had cleared and the company now had in excess of $12,000,000 in the bank which included funds that already belonged to them.

"So many nice round shapes," David replied. "I always did love those oval tones!"

"Don't forget they're sending over their accountant to meet with you at 4:00 pm today," Melanie reminded him.

"Don't worry," he quipped. "You give me money like that and I'll remember everything about you."

Four o'clock rolled around quickly on this fast-paced day. The accountant presented himself at the reception area and was lead into the conference room.

He was offered coffee and sat at the ten foot long conference table eyeing the framed plaques on the walls, waiting for the coffee and the CFO to arrive.

David put on his jacket and went to the conference room to greet the visitor. They performed the customary business card exchange and exchanged pleasantries about the weather and finding the suite in the building.

Melanie went to David's office to bring him a fax that had just come in only to find him not there. She walked down the hall looking into offices hoping to locate him. One of the secretaries offered the information that she thought he was in the conference room. Melanie continued her search and found the secretary was right.

As she entered the conference room, she heard two voices but saw only David's back which blocked the body of the other person from view.

"Sorry to interrupt you, David," Melanie began, "but I wanted you to see this."

As David turned to face her, Melanie was able to see the person standing behind him. David moved aside to clear a path for the introductions which would follow.

The accountant moved toward Melanie with arms extended to embrace her. David's face showed his surprise at this overfriendly reaction. The accountant wrapped his arms around Melanie as David remarked, "Well, I was going to introduce the two of you but you seem to have met!"

"Yes, David, this is my cousin Maisy's husband, Frank," Melanie explained.

CHAPTER FORTY-ONE

MELANIE WAS ANXIOUS to tell Uncle Nate about the amazing coincidence of Frank's appearance at her office that day. When the meeting ended, Melanie checked the time and rushed to her desk to place that call guessing someone would be at home. The phone was answered by Nate.

"Hi Uncle Nate!" Melanie began, breathlessly.

"Hey, Mel," Nate answered, recognizing her voice at once. "How're ya doin'?"

"Just great, just great. I called to tell you something amazing!"

"Tell me about it, Mel. Hilda's at her Golden Giving Guild meeting so I've got lots of time to chat."

"You'll never guess who came to my office today!"

"Who?"

"Frank!"

"Frank? What for?"

Mel explained her company's plans and how Frank was sent representing their new Investment Bankers, RCA &D, to begin their consultation services and the due diligence process. Nate listened without interrupting Melanie, partly from his interest in her remarks and partly from the lack of an appropriate response given his state of shock. Nate's bodily reactions said it all: he broke out in a cold sweat, every muscle in his body contracted, and his heartbeat raced. He did not want to believe what he was hearing. Like a master chess player, Nate's mind skipped at lightning speed from absorbing Melanie's words to grasping the impact of the domino effect of Frank's visit, to focus on the need to contain and minimize the damage to his favorite niece that would surely result from the presence of Frank in Melanie's business life.

Mechanically, Nate acknowledged the coincidence, found reasons to say a quick goodbye and replaced the telephone receiver in its cradle, his body pumping adrenalin as his mind moved into flight mode. It was time to put a stop to RCA&D's plans, whatever they were. Clearly, they could only be up to no good, Nate thought.

Nate walked to the den and blended into his favorite chair which, from years of use, was molded to his form. Nate's mind engaged in assessing the situation. RCA&D's plan was obvious to Nate. Something had to stop that plan from going forward. Nate knew he was the only one who could do that. But what could he do? What could he do?

Hilda returned from her meeting at eleven o'clock to find Nate deep in thought in his favorite chair. All of her urging did not pry him loose. Although Nate said he just wanted to think for a little while and would come to bed soon, the early rays of sunshine crept across Nate's legs bringing the dawn of a beautiful day.

Nate was wide awake. The night had slipped into daybreak unnoticed by Nate. His fixed gaze focused on a blank space on the wall while his mind reviewed the plan he had created during the night. Step by step, Nate had organized in his mind the perfect plan, complete with who would be necessary to make the plan work.

Nate would have to call in his markers. He would need the cooperation, assistance, and the complete confidentiality of old friends from his days on the police force who owed him favors and who, in fact, owed their lives to Nate.

You would never have known that Nate had lost a night's sleep by the way he energetically bounded out of his favorite chair to splash water on his face, grab a cup of coffee and get on the phone.

For efficiency's sake, Nate made a list of those he needed to call. The last time he wrote these names down was for the guest list for Maisy's wedding. As he added the last name to the list, Nate looked over his handiwork with intensity and confidence that this was the team that would make his plan effective. This would work. It had to work. Failure was not an option.

Nate's telemarketing campaign began aimed at the elite group on his list. Each one was specially selected because each met two criteria: each owed his life or the life of a loved one to Nate and each had suffered in some way from something done by RCA&D that could not be prosecuted in a court of law. Each had a personal ax to grind in RCA&D's corporate skull and each would feel justified in implementing a plan to impose vigilante justice.

Every call Nate placed followed the same script as if Nate had written the response himself:

"Hello. This is Nate Goldman. I need a favor."

"Sure, Nate. For you, *anything.*"

And so it began.

Four hours later, Nate had his plan in place. Each man knew what he had to do, when he had to do it, and was committed to pulling off this job. No one had to be told about secrecy or confidentiality. These men were bonded in brotherhood. The deed would be done with the smoothness of skating on ice and professional attention to detail. And it would be done at once, tonight.

CHAPTER FORTY-TWO

THE MORNING AFTER Frank's visit to David King's office, Frank called Maisy before he left the hotel to let her know he'd be on his way back to Bethesda after a quick update meeting at RCA &D's building. Frank left for RCA&D's headquarters early. He had a lot to report to Dugan about David King's company. This was going to be a sweet deal.

Traffic was heavy in the area where RCA&D was located. Frank was glad he got an early start. Even with the traffic delay, he would arrive ahead of schedule. As Frank turned the corner, the RCA&D building came into view. It felt strange coming back for a meeting here. It felt stranger when Frank saw the building surrounded by fire engines. Men in yellow slickers and high boots dragged huge hoses from place to place. Yellow vinyl ribbon stretched around the entire building.

Frank had to park a block away, not being able to reach the company parking lot next to the building. He walked, almost jogged, to the building.

When he arrived at the main entrance, firemen greeted him on the steps. Before Frank could advance any farther, one of the firemen said, "Sorry, sir, no one can enter the building."

"But I've got a meeting," Frank tried to explain.

"You only think you have a meeting," the other fireman quipped. "Only firemen are allowed in. The building is condemned."

"What do you mean by 'condemned?'" Frank asked.

"It means nobody goes in until the fire department decrees it's safe to go in!" the fireman answered authoritatively.

"Well, when do you think that will be?" Frank asked.

"Maybe tomorrow, maybe the next day," he answered, "but, for sure, not now! So move along buddy so these guys behind you can get in to do their job."

"Well, what happened?" Frank persisted.

"Electrical fire. Started in the electrical box. So until the power is restored, the building is designated as condemned and nobody gets in," the fireman emphasized.

The crowd trying to gain entry to the building was turned away from the entrance. The secretaries chattered animatedly and expressed their delight at having the day off. Frank decided to check back into his hotel and stay overnight until he could get together with Dugan for his meeting, rather than making the trip back to Bethesda. Reaching Dugan on his cell phone, Frank confirmed an appointment to meet him midmorning the next day to give Dugan a chance to get to his office and assess any damage.

The next morning, Dugan arrived early. He, too, had been denied entry by the firemen the day before. He was certain he would be able to get in today, even if it was only to get confidential papers, his calendar, and other items in a fire-secure safe. He hoped he would be able to stay at least long enough to do what he needed to do and to meet Frank.

Even though he owned the building, the firemen had the right to keep him out yesterday, a concept he had difficulty grasping. He was sure he would get in this morning.

To his surprise, Dugan was met at the front entrance of his office building by a uniformed band of firemen accompanied by a squadron of police. Before he could say one word, one of the policemen said, "Sorry, sir, no one is allowed inside."

"But I own the building," Dugan snapped back. "And I need to get in to get some of my papers. I have a business to run!"

"Sorry, sir, but there was a burglary here last night and we've got police officers and the Canine Patrol going through the building right now to be certain that none of the burglars is still inside."

"What did they take?" Dugan inquired.

"We won't know until we let everyone in to inventory the offices. But I can tell you that all the glass in the doors is broken and every drawer in every desk and file cabinet is open. But you'll have to wait until we've secured the building to get in," the policeman concluded.

Dugan thanked him and walked away. There was no point in harassing a cop. But he had no intention of being kept out of his own building. He knew another way in.

Walking around to the back of the building where no guard was placed since there was no obvious door, Dugan, unnoticed, removed a stone from the wall, revealing a knob on a safe-like device hidden from view by the stone. Turning the knob activated a gear that made a portion of the wall swing inward, creating a space large enough for Dugan to walk through. The door closed silently on huge hydraulic hinges. Dugan crept quietly up a back stairway, climbing all the way up to the floor where the stairway exited from behind a paneled wall into the hallway near his office.

Without electricity, the area Dugan entered was pitch black. It occurred to him that his lighter, at this moment, was worth a King's ransom. Once in his office, light from windows illuminated the space.

Dugan could see at once that the policeman was right. Everywhere he looked, there were signs of vandalism. Glass and papers were everywhere. What the firemen didn't damage, the burglars did.

It was clear to Dugan that this was a one-two punch of a fire followed by a burglary that was a *message*, not a coincidence, not an unfortunate set of coincidental circumstances.

Dugan walked around surveying the room. Every drawer was open. Surprisingly, upon examination of the contents of his desk drawers and file drawers, it didn't look like anything had been taken. All of the artwork was untouched. There was just enough of a mess to create concern but this was clearly a professional job.

Computers and other valuables were in their places and undamaged. And, most importantly, the paneled wall which hid Dugan's walk-in safe was undisturbed.

Thankfully, all of the documents which Dugan used to control people's lives were in that safe and, indeed, safe behind that wall. There didn't appear to be any fire damage either. Whatever happened was minimal.

Dugan's success was built on attention to detail. Inner compulsion moved him to open the vault to see with his own eyes that his life was, indeed, intact. He twirled the round dial, landing on the appropriate numbers and the paneled wall opened, allowing Dugan to step into the vault. His worst fears were confirmed when his eyes surveyed the vault. Every file drawer was open and empty.

Suddenly, the whole picture fell together for Dugan. The fire was set to keep people, including the night watchman, out of the building so that the "burglars" could get in without worry of detection. The vandalism was done in each office to cover the real reason for the burglar's entry to clean out Dugan's private vault.

As Dugan turned to leave his empty vault, he saw a note on the wall held in place by a pen knife. Dugan reached up, pulled down the note and read it twice before setting fire to it with his lighter.

Dugan got the message. He was just made powerless. The threat of his own documents being held over his head had just brought his world to a crashing halt. It was clear that his life was just thrown into disarray. Power was no longer his. His life was over.

Dugan sat down at his desk, head in hands, deep in thought, trying to comprehend the meaning of the acts of the last 48 hours and their impact on his life. The jumble of thoughts racing through his mind were interrupted by the ringing of his private telephone, the only telephone not linked to the electrically powered voicemail system.

It was difficult to hear the caller because of the deafening noise being generated by one of those pesky commuter helicopters Dugan often observed passing his window. He always wished he had gone to the meetings with the local building owners to protest the rooftop heliport that was installed nearby. With his head filled with so much this morning, this was one distraction he could have done without.

The caller was Frank who had stopped for coffee and wanted to be sure Dugan was there before he drove the rest of the way to the building.

"I tried your cell phone and got no answer," Frank said.

"I was walking up my private stairway," Dugan replied. "There's a lot of concrete there. I'm glad you tried again. Listen, Frank. You won't believe this. Last night there was a burglary in the building and the building is still closed. I sneaked in but the cops won't let you in. I'm the only one in the building except for cops and police dogs. I'm squirreled up in my office but I'm going to sneak back out any minute now. So let me call you later and I'll let you know where to meet me. I'm anxious to hear your report. But let's not discuss it on the phone."

"Yes, sir, Mr. Dugan," Frank replied but Dugan had already hung up.

Frank drove toward the RCA&D building in his company Cadillac with the radio on. A news bulletin interrupted the music:

"This is an update on a crisis situation at the building owned by RCA&D. Police have closed off a large area to traffic. You'll want to avoid the area from Glen Cove Road to Mineola Avenue and from Old Country Road to Northern Boulevard which are now blockaded. All traffic is being detoured from the area. You are advised to take alternate routes to avoid the area. Events of the last 48 hours include a suspicious fire followed by a break-in. The building has been closed and condemned by the fire department since yesterday. Police officers with the Canine Patrol are now in the sealed off building since they suspect a perpetrator may be trapped inside.

"We have just received a report that a police helicopter has spotted a man in one of the upper floor offices who they believe is one of the burglars. We are advised that members of the SWAT team are on board the helicopter," the announcer continued.

Dugan decided he had better get some sensitive files out of his office and retrace his steps back through the secret door before the cops and dogs discovered him. He gathered papers from his desk drawers and from the inbox on his desk.

Frank, hearing the radio announcement was convinced that the man seen by the police helicopter had to be Dugan. He had to warn him to get out of there. Frank called Dugan's private telephone.

The phone rang in Dugan's office. Pushing all the files he was holding into his left arm, Dugan reached across his desk to grab the phone. His movements placed him squarely in front of the window which made him an easy target for the SWAT team. The ground commander signaled the helicopter crew to wound the suspect. Two shots were fired. Only one was necessary to fulfill Nate's dream.

Dugan lay sprawled on the floor of his office with a bullet in his head.

Nate was sitting at the round table that was hugged by the cornering kitchen walls, sipping a cup of freshly brewed coffee, thumbing through Newsday and listening to the radio when the news bulletin cut into the regularly scheduled programming.

"Three terrible events at one building," the announcer explained.

"First, a fire, then a burglary and now the death of the building's owner who was mistaken for a burglar and shot by the police."

Nate heard words like" tragic," "unfortunate," and "untimely" on the news report.

A smile spread over Nate's face.

"Perfect," he thought. "Just perfect. Who could ask for anything more?"

THE END

EPILOGUE

Frank and Maisy moved to Florida to escape the connection to RCA&D and to put space between Hilda and Nate in their daily lives. Frank opened his own accounting firm. He performs background checks on all potential clients before taking them on.

Sylvie and Dave are raising the three children they have had together as well as Jennifer and Joshua, who are now bi-lingual in French and English. Sylvie does not want any live-in help.

David King found other investors. The company survived, unscathed by its numerous meetings with RCA&D. After Allison's death, he turned his attention toward Melanie.

Melanie realized she was not ready to compromise every principle, interest, and desire she had for own life in order to help David reach his goals. She left the firm and focused on philanthropic work and her foundation and spends much of the year traveling. She keeps in touch with David by dropping him post cards, the last of which was postmarked from the South of France.

Rose lived to see Trevor, Jr., graduate from college. She had raised a strong, independent, well-educated, caring man, able to rise above unfairness.

Nate and Hilda, missing their baby girl, Maisy, and wishing to escape northern winters, moved to Florida a year after Frank and Maisy's move. They bought a house within walking distance of Frank and Maisy. Some things never change.

The flowers on the bema at Temple Shalom Lev are still plastic, tacky, and dusty. Some things never change.

# # #